Don Rhodes

Bugs in Amber

A Collection of Short Stories

Matador
9 Priory Business Park,
Wistow Road, Kibworth Beauchamp,
Leicestershire. LE8 0RX
Tel: 0116 279 2299
Email: books@troubador.co.uk
Web: www.troubador.co.uk/matador
Twitter: @matadorbooks

ISBN 978 1784625 436

British Library Cataloguing in Publication Data.
A catalogue record for this book is available from the British Library.

Printed and bound in the UK by TJ International, Padstow, Cornwall
Typeset in 11pt Aldine401 BT by Troubador Publishing Ltd, Leicester, UK

Matador is an imprint of Troubador Publishing Ltd

To my wife, Julie, my sons, Matt and Chris,
and their respective partners, Laura and Becky.

With love, from me, to you.

Contents

The Secret Burial of Richard Middleham

Captain Wilcock now has ample time to reflect on his life on these long winter nights. He got rid of the TV after his wife died. He always unplugs the phone at 6 pm prompt and listens to the news on the radio. After that, the rest of the day is his to read, listen to a little music, to reflect and even to cat nap sometimes, although he's always angry with himself for this indulgence when he snaps awake in his chair.

Together with his wife, Dorothy, he had moved on retirement from a distinguished military career to Sheriff Hutton, a lovely little village outside York. He thinks "distinguished" is not an exaggeration.

Early 1993 it was. The village was their idyll. They had bought a beautiful Georgian house near a lovely old church. They were amongst good people. He quickly became Chairman of the Parish Council, his wife a leading light at the WI. He also became a Church Warden and had taken on organizing funerals for the Vicar.

But twenty years on from their move to the village, life seems somehow different. He feels he hasn't changed at all but things have slowly changed around him. He can't pinpoint when he first began to notice intrusions from the outside world into his beloved Sheriff Hutton. At first these were just irritations. Wind turbines looming down from nearby hills, dwarfing the ancient oaks in the fields below. Satellite dishes are another eyesore. Fixing them to York-stone houses is like sticking a red plastic nose on the Mona Lisa. And the proliferation of so-called street furniture disfigures every view.

He used to grumble to Dorothy every time he spotted some new sign warning of a danger that only the health and safety Gestapo could see:

"There'll be a sign telling us to '*Beware distracting street signs*' soon, Dorothy. You watch!"

"Oh. Calm down," she'd giggle. "It's progress. You'll get used to it."

But now, she's not here to calm him down anymore. And he hasn't got used to it. He gets even angrier.

But there's one much bigger threat to the way of life he loves...the fact that absolutely no one in public life knows how to behave any more. Not MPs grubbing around in the expenses trough. Not this new breed of spiv-bankers. Not the journalists who hacked the phone of a murdered schoolgirl. Not lying policemen, who believe themselves above the law. Not public servants, brazenly explaining away scandalous negligence. Not the government with its endless double-speak.

It really does make him wonder whether the sacrifices of the men of Fighter and Bomber Command and of those on the Normandy beaches have been worth it after all.

No-one seems prepared to stand up for what's right anymore. For the UK in an ungrateful Europe. For England within the UK, where we let those jumped-up Scottish and Welsh county councils...he refuses to call them parliaments...grant themselves privileges that the English fund but don't enjoy.

Since Dorothy's death, these trends have troubled him more and more. He was always cool under fire so he conceals his anger well. But he has begun to worry just how strong this anger is. He may appear to others much the same as ever but he knows something powerful is churning below the surface, daily harder to contain.

He is by nature and training a man of action. He feels the need to act now, make a stand, do something, anything to dissipate the anger. The veneer that holds all his resentments in place is cracking. What on earth will emerge if it fractures completely? It frightens him a little. He shuffles in his chair, as if a change in posture will snap him out of it but he is too agitated to go to bed until the early hours.

« »

So the past has gradually become a more comfortable place than the present for Captain Wilcock. He tends to spend more and more of his time there. The Captain travels into York every third Wednesday of the month, when he spends the morning at his Medieval History Group, lunches with a former comrade and then passes the afternoon at the regimental museum.

Today, his history group is discussing a topical item. Such items help to show, their leader Beatrice feels, that medieval history is still alive for them.

"Oh do get on with it, Beatrice," the Captain thinks but is much too polite to say.

She suggests that they write a collective letter to the press supporting the proposal that the recently discovered remains of King Richard III be brought to York for re-burial after five hundred years in a car park in Leicester.

They brainstorm…not a phrase the Captain has ever used …the case for a re-burial in York. This is easy for this group of committed Yorkists.

Someone starts with:

"Richard has always been loved in York, unlike elsewhere in England!"

"He has no connection with Leicester other than that he happened to die there" is the second argument.

"Yes, and who'd want to stay in Leicester? Anyone been? Awful place!"

This is not recorded.

"Well said! And "finders-keepers" is hardly a principle of English law."

Other, points come thick and fast:

"He was married in York Minster…"

"He lived many years at Middleham in Yorkshire…"

"He ruled the North for the King, his brother, and did it very well, too."

"Yes, and Richard's son, Edward, Prince of Wales, has a cenotaph in Sheriff Hutton church…Oh, and he was crowned Prince in York Minster."

"Richard gifted the Minster money and was funding the establishment of a Chantry Chapel in York…"

"...yes, that's evidence that he intended to be buried there!"

"Numerous blood relatives have stated he should be returned to York for burial. That should count for a lot."

A rarely-heard, very Yorkshire voice booms in and silences the hubbub:

"He disliked the south and it disliked him."

The south is anywhere below Sheffield and so clearly includes Leicester. The booming voice continues:

"Northerners and folk in York especially have always loved him. It's a tragedy he's been in exile so long and been treated so bad. Crammed into a shallow grave in a car park! Honestly. They're not fit to have him! They only want to make a show of him to pull in tourists. People who don't know Richard III from Robin Hood, standing in line and gawping at a plaster cast of his spine. Taking pictures with their Japanese cameras and phones. It's a disgrace. It's just not right."

There's a pause followed by a slow, deliberate:

"We should do something about it."

Captain Wilcock's ears prick up at this point. This has all been delivered with passion by Bill Wainwright, a retired undertaker, who has said little at any previous meeting but is always a brooding presence with his bushy eyebrows and big, raw-boned frame. He really means this though. It scares the others slightly.

Beatrice is clearly uncomfortable with such strong feeling. She regains control by proposing that she turn the ideas into a "well-crafted letter" to be sent to the press on behalf of the group.

There's only one dissenting voice, Bill's:

"No offence, Beatrice, but letters won't do any good, well-crafted or not. It's action we need. We should go and get 'im. We should bring King Richard 'ome."

The rest of the group laughs, nervously, because they are not sure whether Bill means it or not. Captain Wilcock doesn't laugh. He sneaks a look at the list of members' contact details. It's meant to encourage networking between sessions. "Networking" is another word the Captain dislikes but in this instance he'll make an exception. Network he will.

« »

"Did you mean it, Bill?" the Captain asks when he surprises Bill Wainwright with a call that night.

"Every word," Bill replies.

"Including the 'bring him home' bit?"

"Especially the 'bring 'im 'ome' bit. That more than anything."

"Do you think we could do it…just the two of us?"

"Well he's not that heavy any more. He won't have his armour on you know."

The Captain thinks this is a joke but with Bill it's hard to tell.

"Anyway, I've lifted some porkers in my time I can tell you, Captain. And I've kept my 'and in 'elping my son out. I've still got access to a nice hearse and a lovely coffin. A coffin fit for a king."

"It's more the security side of things. It can't be easy to break into a morgue as you'll no doubt know."

"Except he's not in a morgue. He's at the university. In the Archaeology Department. If we can't outsmart a few G4S men we don't deserve to succeed."

"You've thought about this, Bill, I can tell. Let's meet, tomorrow. Can you get over here? We'll not be disturbed at my place. Don't tell another soul, not even your wife."

"Can't tell 'er Captain. I buried 'er myself ten years ago."

Is this another joke? The Captain goes quiet.

"Not under the patio. All legal and proper, Captain… See you tomorrow. I know where you live."

The Captain goes to bed with his head fizzing with ideas. It will be the start of a fight-back, almost a crusade for doing the right thing. They just have to work out now the right way to do the right thing, starting with where to put Richard once he is back in the North. Where indeed?

« »

The next night, Bill and the Captain sip their whiskey and water in the study at Sheriff Hutton. It's late but they've made good progress. The Captain summarizes their plan:

"You can provide a hearse and body bag; we'll transfer the King's remains to an oak coffin once we are back here;

I've ordered a grave to be dug in a quiet spot in Sheriff Hutton graveyard;

We act overnight on the weekend of 23rd and 24th of

February. There'll be no one about in Sheriff Hutton by the time we get back;

I'll put together an order of service, brief but dignified, based on battlefield burials. We can expect a more fitting ceremony at a later date when people come to appreciate that this is where Richard belongs;

We should both put our affairs in order before 23rd February because our lives won't be our own afterwards;

When arrested, we accept responsibility but not guilt;

We will conduct our own defence when we finally appear in court.

Agreed, Bill?"

Bill raises his glass and with a rare smile agrees: "Captain. Let's do it!"

« »

In the bedroom of a modern flat in the suburbs of Leicester in the early hours one February morning, a mobile phone intrudes on an assignation. It's Detective Superintendant Johnson's mobile:

"Johnson here. What time do you call this for God's sake?"

His colleague, Sergeant Finch, is on the other end of the phone:

"It's urgent, Guv. I know it's late and you've got company but, well…you've just got to get yourself down here. Now! The Chief Constable wants to see you. This minute. Sooner if possible… Someone's nicked Richard III! Can you believe it?"

Silence. Finch continues:

"He's asked for you specifically."

"Why would Richard III ask for me, Finch? I hardly know the guy. And he's dead so he's not asking for anybody. This is a wind-up, right? You're pulling my leg. Finch, are you recording this? Am I on speaker? You'll be back in uniform before the week's out, you arsehole!"

"I am not winding you up, Boss. Trust me. Some bastard's nicked Richard III. Really. The Chief Constable's livid. He refused to provide security for the body. He said the University had to do it themselves. G4S got the job and they've messed up, big time! The Chief thinks he'll be a laughing stock. He overheard some of us in CID rehearsing all the possible headlines. I thought he was going to have a bloody heart attack."

More silence. Finch is desperate:

"Get yourself down here or your life won't be worth living. You'll be in that vacant hole in the car park and nobody will come looking for you, believe me. Well, not for another five hundred years or so…Sir"

Johnson finally swings his legs out of bed.

There's further movement under the crumpled duvet. Cindy, his occasional overnight guest, is not pleased:

"You don't have to go, surely! First time for ages I manage a night away from you-know-who and you're buggering off. What sort of a way is that to treat a girl?"

"Girl? If you say so…"

She throws a book from the bedside table at him as he disappears into the bathroom.

"Ouch! That's my bedtime reading you've just hit me with. Look. I'm sorry! I really am. But I've got to go. Something's come up. The Chief's going to brief me personally in thirty minutes…"

"What is it? Come on. Tell Cindy! There has to be *some* reward for screwing a Detective Superintendant. I haven't found much else. All this secrecy. It's not as if I'll tweet it or anything. What is it?"

Johnson thinks for a minute.

"Well. It'll be all over the media in a few hours anyway. Just don't tell that husband of yours! Can't trust a journo. He's suspicious enough as it is. It's Richard III. Someone's nicked him. Well, nicked his skeleton to be accurate. I've got to find him…it, or else…"

He grabs his mobile and keys from the bedside table.

"Let yourself out. I'll ring you…Mum's the word!"

« »

The Chief Constable paces up and down his cavernous office during the entire briefing:

"It's obviously a highly professional group of criminals. International probably, working on a commission for some super-rich client. Not Arab. Too much respect for religion, the Arabs. Perhaps a reclusive American heritage-freak. No, probably Russian. Yes, laundered money from Russia."

That's easy then, Johnson thinks. I'll just get out my file on *Russian super-rich weirdoes with a fetish involving dead Plantagenet kings. Volume 1*. It can't be that thick.

He doesn't say any of this. He just nods agreement and showily takes notes of the Chief's drivel, notes that he will bin as soon as he's out of the room.

The Chief rambles on:

"They knew exactly what they were doing. In and out in 30 minutes, whilst the guard was distracted by noises elsewhere. And the technical skill in bi-passing the alarms. Military in its execution. Oh, yes…the only bit of CCTV we have shows the suspects wearing old people masks. As if we'd be fooled by a few latex wrinkles. I ask you!"

He goes on:

"The Archaeology Department at the University can offer specialist and technical advice. Yes, and on possible markets for the skeleton of a dead English King. Any problems or backsides need kicking, come to me. No loose talk from any of your officers. Your team must be tight as… " He stalls. He is struggling to finish his simile with a word that fit the new guidelines on political correctness he's just issued. "a..a… tight as a tick!"

It makes about as much sense as anything else he's said already.

That's the "helpful" bit from the Chief Constable. The rest is more menacing:

"Johnson. We need a result on this. And quickly. There's a lot resting on it. Don't let me down…" "Or else!" he means but doesn't say.

"No Sir. I'll get on with it right away. Thank you, Sir."

Johnson nods and leaves the room, not backwards but almost.

« »

In the tea-time edition of the Leicester Mail that day, James Adamson, a local journalist, has broken the story ahead of local rivals and the red-tops. He is lauded back in his news room but leaves early to try to find out from his wife Cindy how she knew about the robbery.

He confronts his wife in the kitchen of their home as she prepares a light supper:

"Never mind whether the headline was naff or not, how did you know that Richard had been stolen hours before even the red-tops got it? Where were you last night anyway? Not staying at your parents as you said. I thought you'd stopped seeing him, your frigging Inspector Clouseau."

Cindy has her back to him and is looking out of the window:

"Superintendant, actually. But you lot at the Mail never did get the accuracy thing, did you? And anyway, it's a good job I look out for stories for you. You don't come up with many yourself. This is the first scoop you've had since … how long is it? Two years? Three? Or was it Richard's death at Bosworth, 1485 wasn't it, your last scoop!"

James fumes.

"Anyway," she goes on, "the headline *was* naff. I wouldn't have bloody-well bothered if I'd known that the best you could do was:

He's behind you!

Leicester Pantomime Season Continues.

Good God. It must have taken the combined brains of the Leicester Mail all of ten seconds to come up with that one. Pantomime's the right word!"

"I don't do the headlines as you know. And I'd rather do without a scoop than have my wife sleep with half of Leicestershire CID to get it…"

She turns to face him, arms folded, back against a worktop:

"Don't exaggerate…These things happen. We're all adults. Well most of us. And anyway, is it any worse than some of the ways your lot gets a story? Don't you dare lecture me! I haven't hacked anyone's phone. Or door-stepped grieving parents. Or bribed policemen for information."

She pauses.

"Well. That last one may not be strictly true."

James moves to within a few inches of her, just about nose-to-nose but she doesn't flinch.

"That's it for me. End. Finito! You can pack your bags… And I'm going to sort him out, your Keystone Cop! I'll bide my time but I'll sort him, don't you worry. Prat! CID…gang of fucking laager louts!

He turns and leaves for the Chief Constable's evening press conference.

« »

The conference is packed. The Chief Constable sits looking confident but he hates these events, loathes these smart-arse journalists. They think coming up with slick questions is a gift when it's coming up with answers that's the real talent. Anyway, he'll just have to get through it and get back to the real job, nicking villains. The event is to be chaired by Joceline Saunders, his PR Director.

After a brief presentation of what everybody already knows, Joceline kicks off the Q&A session:

"The Chief Constable will take a few questions now… You, Sir. Second from the left, front row…"

"Hi, Chief Constable. Mark Rogers, London Times…"

The Chief Constable shuffles in his chair with irritation. He's not a "Hi" sort of chap.

"… do you regret the decision not to provide a guard for King Richard? Is your force incapable of providing proper security for our royalty? Would the Queen be safe if she visited Leicester on your watch?"

My God, the Chief thinks. An Oxbridge education and that's the best he can do, sitting there smug with his grinning cronies all around him.

"I'm pleased you've asked me that. Of course Her Majesty would be safe! We have an excellent record on royal protection…"

Rogers interrupts the Chief:

"…with respect, Richard himself might have a different view, Chief Constable."

Joceline intervenes:

"I think the Chief Constable has answered your question. Next question please. You. Third from the end, next to back row. Yes. You…"

"Maggie Holmes, Yorkshire Post. Has Leicester forfeited the right to keep Richard's remains in future because of your force's negligence? Always assuming Richard is found again, of course. It did take rather a long time to find him last time he went missing."

"Richard's ultimate resting place is clearly not a matter for me as Chief Constable. We are concentrating all our efforts on finding his remains and of course the perpetrators of this dreadful crime. I can report that we are making excellent progress and as you would expect I have placed the full resources of the force at the disposal of the officer in charge of the case, a most capable detective."

Joceline comes in again:

"James. Your turn. Maybe a local angle?"

"James Adamson, Leicester Mail. Speaking of the officer in charge, have you confidence that nothing is leaking from his team? There were whispers locally about the theft very early…almost as soon as it had happened in fact."

Warm, re-assurance is one of the Chief's strengths:

"I have very faith in the DS in charge of the case. I briefed him personally. He is a man of tremendous standing in police circles, a highly energetic officer…"

James Adamson issues a barely audible:

"So I believe…"

"…he's already making progress. Good progress," the Chief adds.

"So what leads are you working on, Chief Constable," the Times man asks.

"Well, obviously I can't reveal too much. These are early days still. But let me assure you…the tentacles of Leicestershire Constabulary are already reaching to all corners of the world in this global enquiry. No doubt we are dealing with sophisticated international criminals here but have no fear, we will hunt them down to the Middle East or Russia or wherever they hide. We will pursue them relentlessly and bring them to justice. Yes, to justice here in Leicester."

"So, in short," Rogers says, "you've no idea where Richard is, Chief Constable? He could be anywhere. Have you eliminated the possibility of a historical motivation here? Say a Yorkist connection?

"What tosh! Absolutely not!"

Joceline looks alarmed at the Chief's firmness but he ploughs on.

"All our extensive forensic analysis and, I might add, my old-fashioned copper's instincts tell me that these thieves are international big-timers with a ready buyer for these artefacts. It's about money. Dirty profit from crime, not some centuries old argument that most people have forgotten about. Trust us. We know criminals. We know crime. Leave the investigation to us. We know what we're doing…"

A hand goes up in the middle.

"Mandy Brown, Sky News. We received a report this afternoon that your team has used SUS laws to stop and search a funeral cortege on its way to the Leicester crematorium. The mourners were made to stand with their hands on the top of the hearse while the coffin was searched. The footage is on YouTube. Was that based on forensic analysis or on your old-fashioned copper's instincts?"

The Chief is rattled.

"What? Can't be! I know nothing about that. Nothing at all...You can't repeat unconfirmed speculation."

Joceline comes to his aid:

"That's all we have time for! The Chief Constable is a very busy man, as you'll appreciate."

Slight as she is, Joceline heaves the Chief up from his chair and ushers him out. As they make for the door, there are final attempts to ask the Chief questions:

"Have you carried out dawn raids on any undertakers yet?"

"I've heard you've engaged a Medium, Chief Constable. Any truth in that rumour?"

"Will you be you excavating any more car parks?"

« »

Johnson is obviously under ever mounting pressure to "get a result", as policemen and football managers say nowadays. Motivated entirely by self preservation, he's eliminated the Chief's theories first, even though he knew they were pure bullshit. First he'd alerted the airports and foreign police forces to be on the look-out for career criminals and their skinny co-traveller. Nothing. The Chief's archaeology experts and the Antiques Road

Show guys hadn't a clue. A few Meissen figures were the limit of their expertise. The CCTV had led nowhere.

His own efforts have hardly been more effective. None of his local informants know anything. The G4S guys were simply inept, not in on the heist. The North Yorkshire police have picked up no Yorkist plot to hijack Richard's remains.

He hasn't slept since the news broke. He's even had to raid the evidence store for some amphetamine to keep him going. It looks like the end of the road. Back on traffic for him.

As one last throw of the dice, he books a call to the Russian Security Police in Moscow. It takes a while until they find someone who can speak English but eventually he's put through to a Lieutenant Vladimir Gromyko.

Gromyko is very direct:

"What's all the fuss about a few royal bones? You are sentimental fools, you British."

"Well, they're important to us. We really need you to look out for them. I'll send you photos and a description."

He notices that his voice sounds tinny. Gromyko has put him on speaker for his comrades to hear the crazy Englishmen banging on about a few old bones.

"No need," Gromyko says. "We know what bones look like."

His mates are guffawing by this time. There might even be a bit of thigh-slapping.

"People go missing all the time here in Russia. We know where most of them are but we don't tell anyone.

Wait a few seconds, friend Johnson. Just a moment…"

Gromyko speaks some Russian, followed by the sound of departing boots. He clicks Johnson back off speaker. His voice drops to a whisper and the sarcasm is gone:

"Hey, Johnson. We can…how you say… snip a deal here. Good deal for both of us."

"Cut a deal, actually. It's unlikely but go on anyway."

"Well. Cut? Snip? Same deal. We have lots of Royal bones here. A church full of them in St Petersburg. I can organise a delivery. Royal bones, too. Top quality. You tell me required size, small, medium or large? Boy bones I suppose. You can claim they are this *Reekard* of yours. They would be Romanov bones. No proletarians. They were related to your lot so they'd even do ok in DNA test. What do you say, friend Johnson? One hundred K sterling."

Johnson hangs up. He feels very alone and very tired. His head drops forward onto the desk. He bangs it gently a few times and then lets it rest there.

« »

Johnson's head is still on his desk an hour after his chat with Gromyko when he is woken by the insistent ring of his telephone. It's not Interpol or the FBI or the Russian FSB. It isn't any of the Chief's experts.

It's a Desk Sergeant from Sheriff Hutton. He's just had a call from the village vicar to say his handyman, Jim Briggs, had turned up to clear leaves from the graveyard after lunch that day. He was gobsmacked to see that a newly-dug grave had been filled a week before the date scheduled for the burial of some mystery-man, some Richard Middleham fellow. Jim had run to fetch the Vicar. They'd both stood opened-mouthed at the inscription at the head of the mound of fresh earth:

Here lie the Mortal Remains of King Richard III
Plantagenet King of England
2/10/1452 to 22/8/1485
May He Rest in Peace amongst His Own

"Are you interested?" the Desk Sergeant asks.

Johnson is out of the door in no time, screaming for a car to take him to Sheriff Hutton, wherever that is. The finger of suspicion is already pointing at whoever organises burials at Sheriff Hutton church.

« »

Captain Wilcock is not remotely shocked by the words emerging from the mouth of the man facing him:

"Captain James Henry Wilcock, I am arresting you on suspicion of theft of the mortal remains of King Richard III in Leicester sometime between the 23rd and 24th of February 2013."

The detective gallops through the caution. Captain Wilcock waits patiently for him to finish. Those who know the Captain's good manners would have predicted the first half of his response:

"Come in please, Officer. Come in out of the cold."

They would probably not have predicted the second half:

"I've been expecting you."

Detective Superintendant Johnson and another officer from the Leicestershire Constabulary follow Captain Wilcock into his home. Two uniformed constables stand guard at the door.

Neighbours at their twitching curtains in the quiet, elegant street in Sheriff Hutton near York assume at that point that the visit must be about some untoward event that needs the Captain's attention, perhaps to identify a relative's body after a sudden death. They are wrong but not completely. It doesn't concern identification of a body at all. The identification of the body in question was completed much earlier, not by the conventional means of the drawn-back sheet and a nod from a tearful relative. It was done by carbon-dating, archaeological analysis and DNA testing.

The identity of the body is no longer at issue. The issues now are:

Who was involved?

Why have they done it?

Soon a forensics van crawls up the quiet street, stops in front of 10 Church View and disgorges its team of overall-clad officers. Shortly after that, news vans with satellite dishes block the narrow streets. Pushy journalists appear from nowhere and start knocking on doors and asking impertinent questions about the Captain. By this point, even the citizens of this quiet village can be in no doubt that this is more than a notification of a fatal road traffic accident. Something very odd is happening in their village, where a change in refuse-collection day causes consternation. In his wish to protect their way of life, Captain Wilcock has unwittingly inflicted this most frightful intrusion on his beloved village.

« »

On the day of the hearing, the Crown Court building in York is besieged by the world's press. Their appetite for background on the accused has been sharpened by the refusal of the good people of Sheriff Hutton to talk about their unlikely law-breaker.

Once the court proceedings have begun, the Captain knows how annoyed the judge is that he is personally conducting a joint defence of himself and a defiant Bill Wainwright. This has added to the air of English eccentricity so loved by the foreign press.

Captain Wilcock's first tactic is to refuse to enter a plea. He disputes that a crime has been committed. On the theft charge, he argues that human remains, especially those of a monarch, cannot *belong* to anybody. How, he asks, can they be accused of permanently depriving someone of something they do not actually own? Absurd!

He glosses over the criminal damage to the university building. It is a minor matter compared with the fate of the remains of the last Plantagenet King of England. He simply offers to pay for any repair. He brandishes his cheque-book and asks how much he owes. It is, he says, well worth it to see the right thing done.

The gallery loves it. The press artists scribble away, stretching their necks to get a better view. He's quite enjoying himself in a way that he hasn't for years.

The judge, however, is not impressed and talks of "histrionics unworthy of the solemnity of the proceedings."

The Captain refuses absolutely to concede that Bill and he are guilty. He explains, much to the further irritation of the judge but to the amusement of most others, that one can only be guilty of a wrongful act. They have actually put right a long-standing wrong. He treats them to all the arguments for re-burial in York. He knows them by heart. He believes them. A few people mumble agreement. There is the odd "Hear! Hear!"

The judge threatens to empty the court if there is more: "This is not reality TV! There is no audience participation!"

In summary, the Captain accepts that Bill and he have carried out the re-burial and so they are *responsible*, but they are certainly not *guilty*.

The judge orders a "Not Guilty Plea" to be entered.

The prosecution trots through its case. The Captain doesn't contest what has actually happened. It's all true. He knows. He was there. He uses the time to rehearse his final address.

Eventually, having been found guilty, they are invited to offer mitigation. Although the Captain denies there's anything to mitigate, the judge still lets him speak one final time.

He stands up. He pauses until everyone is silent. He launches into the speech that he has fashioned behind the closed curtains of his study:

"Thank you, Your Honour. I'll be brief… In essence, the motivation for our actions arises from the shameful difference between what Richard deserves, and how he has been treated. Most historians agree that in his short reign Richard introduced many far-sighted reforms. I will not repeat them all here. Most A-Level history students know them well. But having achieved so much for his countrymen, we must turn to how he was treated. Was he lauded for these deeds? Was he carried shoulder high through the cheering crowds of London? Well, Your Honour, he was not. His reward was rebellion, humiliation and death."

"And what of plans for him now? Will they redress this injustice? Again the answer is no. As things stand, Richard will be buried in Leicester, almost certainly against the wishes he himself had for his burial. His burial will be in a Cathedral, which, worthy as it is, looks like a modest Parish Church compared to the grandeur of York Minster. I'm sorry, but that's the truth. There has been much squabbling over the design of Richard's tomb. It seems he will have to see out eternity in something described as "modern". But, fear not. He will be honoured by a Visitor Centre nearby. How regal! A visitor centre, like they have at some waxworks or bird sanctuary. One of the exhibits has him in hideous white armour looking, I have it on good authority, like Darth Vader from Star Wars. That presumably is what the focus groups said would appeal to the widest possible audience, an audience that mostly thinks the Richard they are going to see is Richard the Lion Heart, the man who robbed the rich in Sherwood Forest."

There's some suppressed laughter but a few in the public gallery just look bemused.

"The final indignity will be the inevitable glass case containing a plaster cast of Richard's spine. One wonders if the Visitor Centre Trustees would be happy to have representations of their own bunions, varicose veins or haemorrhoids on display to the tourists lining up with their cameras."

"That is how Richard has been treated by the countrymen and women he served so well. We should hang our heads in shame."

The Captain slowly scans the courtroom. One by one, people look down, away, fiddle in their pockets or bags, anything but look into his fierce gaze.

The judge intervenes:

"Could I remind you, Captain Wilcock, that it is you and Mr Wainwright, not the public who are on trial. Please proceed to your conclusion or I will deliver mine."

"I'm nearly done, Your Honour. Nearly done."

He rocks on his heels and continues:

"History will judge us, not this court and not this judge."

His Honour shuffles in his seat.

"In this country," he continues, "injustice never lasts forever. We British have developed in our way of life an innate self-righting mechanism. This is sometimes slow. It may take half a millennium but it never fails to see right eventually conquer wrong. Our sense of fairness means that in time, King Richard III will inevitably be seen as a good, even great monarch."

He pauses again. He stands erect, arms by his side, eyes forward.

"Any man killed in battle, high-bred or low, slain in Bosworth or in Basra, is brought home with love and honour and buried as he and his family wish. Richard should be no exception. That is the service we have done for our former King. Responsible, certainly. Guilty, no. Never!"

The Captain turns to the judge:

"Your Honour, our consciences are clear. Do what you must. Do your worst."

He does.

« »

As he is taken down after sentence, Captain Wilcock glances over at the gallery. Everyone is gazing at him. He spots his old adversary, DS Johnson, and their three eyes lock. Johnson smiles and winks at him from his one good eye. The other is closed with as big and ugly a black eye as the Captain has ever seen, incurred he assumes in the line of duty.

Brief Encounters

My name is...No. You don't need to know my name. I am Roma and you are not. You're a Gadjo. So we don't need names.

I'm a girl. I'm eleven. I think it's eleven. Mama and Papa argue about it:

"She's nine. Nearly ten. Born the autumn after we left Ulmeni," Mama says softly, trying not to provoke him. "I should know her age. I was there at the birth. You were away, working. Anyway, she's too young to be begging on her own."

"She's eleven, I tell you," he snaps back. "Look at her! Of course she's old enough to do stuff on her own. She's eleven. That's that. I'll look after her. I look after you all, don't I?"

Mama doesn't answer but I know what she thinks. She already told me Papa never brought much money back from his working trips but she doesn't mention that either.

This is a typical day for me. I'm resting at the moment out of the way, sitting on my haunches with my back against a wall. I'm in the big square in Prague. The Old Town Square your people call it. I'm in my begging clothes. I have a nice set of clothes for special days. They were my sister's but she ran off with a boy last year so I got them.

I hate my begging clothes but they're what I wear most days. They look dirty but they're not. They're just old. Mama says I can't look smart or people won't give but I must always be clean. That's the Roma way.

I hold my Starbuck's cup loosely in my hand. A few coppers cover the bottom. Although I'm resting out of the way, I shake the cup at passers-by if they come near enough. It's been a bad day. I have to keep trying. There was a heavy shower earlier and it's only just cleared so the square is now filling up.

Look at those people in the cafe over there. Red faces. Filling their padded chairs. Smug, sipping their cream-topped coffees after lunch. It's still only 12:15 by the clock on the square. A bit of salad might have done them more good. Or a fasting day, like we sometimes have in bad times. On days when it's raining, only few Gadje are about and nobody will stop to give to a Roma.

They're blathering away again now, those cafe people. They've already forgotten their brush with me. They weren't so smug a while ago when I appeared from nowhere and reached over the low barrier:

"Can you spare some change for a hungry Gypsy girl?"

I rested one hand on their table and shoved my cup under their noses. I spoke to them in turn:

"Please lady. Just a few coins."

Silence.

I gave her husband the big brown-eyed stare and flicked my lashes:

"Please, Sir. Just those few coins beside your plate."

He didn't respond to me but spoke to his friends:

"God in Heaven! She speaks better German than me. No slang Deutsch for her."

I shook my cup at them in turn, gently at first but harder the tighter that their lips pursed.

Disgust. That's how most Gadje react. Or anger. They can be nasty to me. Yes, even to me, a spindly child, not much higher than their waists. Some of them seem to hate me just for being there, in their world. They feel superior because they've got so much.

He turned to me: "Where are your parents? Why don't *they* feed you? Sitting around smoking and drinking somewhere, I suppose. Try working for a living, like I've always done. All my life."

Well, he wasn't working today. I was. I wanted to ask if he thought trudging the cobbled streets of Prague and Bucharest, being spat at, pushed and even hit was an easy way to earn a living but I didn't.

His friends were embarrassed. Everyone in the cafe was looking at them but he just looked away from me and resumed his conversation, as if I were invisible. The waiter came and shooed me away like he'd shoo away a mangy cat.

Now I'm resting twenty metres or so from the cafe. I notice a man from another small group is looking over at me. "What are you staring at?" I mutter under my breath. I stare him out. He turns back to the conversation with his friends. He must have said something about me because all the others look my way. I give them the eye, too. They're no threat. They are couples mainly. I guess they're English.

Men sometimes look at me funny, sneakily, when they think their wives aren't watching. Mama has warned me about these men. She says they're looking for the shape in my body:

"When men look you up and down, be wary, especially when they're drunk. Don't hang around too long and never go off with one, choose what they offer you. Never!"

It's hard sometimes. Hard to know if they've been drinking or not. Or hard not to chance it when I've had a bad day and hardly covered the bottom of my cup with coins.

"Better avoid men on their own!" Mama says. "They're trouble. Remember! I'll always be within shouting distance. Call in Roma. I'll know it's you."

She's right. Men on their own can be difficult. They sometimes reach out and stroke my cheek or hair. I pull away, even if I lose money by it. I don't want to be made unclean by their touch. But she's never too far off, working away herself with Ana swaddled to her.

Not everybody reacts in these ways. Some give. A lot sometimes. That's how we live and eat.

I need to keep alert, watchful for police or youths that would taunt me or try to steal my takings.

A young, smiley couple come out of their way to put some coins in my cup.

"Merci beaucoup," I say.

"De rien!" the man replies, shocked that I know they're French before they've spoken a word.

I like to surprise them with my little tricks. It's a sense I've got. I'm always right. I know most of their nationalities from just looking. I can spot them and put them in their place.

Papa says not to feel bad about begging:

"Remember...you're doing them a service. A big service! They give you something and they feel good. It makes them feel better. Superior! Big timers! They should have to pay for that service. That's how it works. They shouldn't expect something for nothing."

He knows the best ways to get money out of Gadje:

"Make sure you visit all the churches. They are good ground for us. They're already in the right mood. Near their churches, it's harder for them to look away. They think God's watching them."

Back in the cafe, the English couples are talking to their waiter. One of the men reads so loudly from a travel book that I can make out what he's saying even from here:

"Dalsi dve piva!...Hey, what's 'please' Jim? Quick. Look it up."

The waiter helps him out: "Prosim. It's prosim."

"So," the man shouts, mechanically and louder than ever. "Dalsi dve piva prosim! Prosim!"

"Two more beers? Right away sir," the waiter replies, wheels away and returns inside.

The man who ordered sits back and pours the last drops of beer into his smug mouth.

How clever he feels! Managing to order beer in Czech, reading from a guide-book while the server waits and tries to look impressed.

World travellers! Citizens of the World! Pah! I've travelled most of Eastern Europe and down into the Balkans, and now back to Prague. In ancient cars. In lorries. On laden buses. Slinking over borders at night. Forever in the wrong place. In other people's place. Not really safe. Always being moved on. But never really finding *our* place. We Roma don't have one, unless it's somewhere you Gadje don't want. A rubbish tip. Or land by an open sewer.

Papa says: "Don't worry. Everywhere is our place!"

But it's only really ours to slink around in. Not to own. Never a place to lord it in, like you do.

It makes me angry. I want to spit. At eleven … (I think it's eleven)… I can already beg in ten languages: my own Roma, Romanian, Hungarian, Polish, Serbian and now Czech; all the countries I've travelled through on my journey west. The ten also includes a bit of German, Dutch, French and English.

I know "Poor thing! Why isn't she in school?" and "Are those lice? Tell her to 'eff off!" in five languages. Well, to be honest, the "eff off" is only ever in English.

I've never had lice. You Gadje are the dirty ones. You don't know how to keep clean like we do.

I can't read or write in any language. That doesn't bother me. I don't *write* to them for money. I don't always need to speak. My clothes and my look talk for me: "Give me something! You'll feel better and I'll go away."

I stand up for a better view. I want to keep the cafe clientele in view because when it changes a bit more, I'll try another visit.

So who's the clever one, me or them?

I sometimes have fun by speaking gobbledy-gook as I push my cup under their noses:

"Dotsy, minkle parvi miesch, por favor."

"Pardon?" they say.

"Mucho dotsy, minkle parvi miesch, por favour, Sir."

Someone will think they've worked out what I'm saying. Clever that is as I'm saying nothing. Zilch. Nichts. Rien. Nic. Nimic. Nothing!

It's usually a woman: "She wants money. She said something about not having eaten for days. Give her something, Hansi. Poor thing."

A few coppers tumble into my cup. I don't thank them. Not in gobbledy-gook or any language because they don't expect that from Roma.

I wish I could take the weight off my feet.

Another thing I sometimes do with the westerners is to say something rude to them in Roma. Something like:

"Give me money, fatso. You've obviously got plenty or that wife of yours wouldn't stay with a porker like you."

If I say it with the right look, this is just as good as a heartfelt plea or a limp.

It's dangerous to try it with locals though. They know the odd Roma word. They have hard enough lives themselves and we're all after the same money. So we give the locals a wide berth unless they're coming out of church.

Day to day, locals are dangerous, especially when staggering home drunk. We are quicker though and it's easy to keep a distance from a lumbering, lone Czech drunk. The gangs are different. But we know their streets better than they do. We know when to disappear into the shadows until Papa comes and picks us up.

Mmm. Two municipal guards heading my way. Better disappear for a while…

« »

This is much worse than hanging about in the Old Town Square every day. I've been sitting at home for a week, drawing in the dust with a stick outside our hut on the camp. My brothers and sisters are playing inside, getting on Mama's nerves as she cleans up yet again. I'm keeping watch.

We are all going slowly crazy. The hunger doesn't help. Papa's really jumpy. Every time a strange car drives through the camp, he disappears. I'm meant to warn him if I see strangers approaching.

It's usually police looking for someone or something. As if we can't spot their stupid faces, in or out of uniform.

They come slowly and too obviously to catch anyone off guard.

Papa knows who they're after. Me and Mama know who they're after. The whole camp knows who they're after. It's him, Papa. I'm afraid.

So we can't go out begging. Others from the camp have tried, just to test things out, but the atmosphere in the city is tense. People bristle as we approach them. They're not just full of hate. They're scared as well. So we stay cooped up on the camp, scratching around in the dust alongside our scrawny chickens. Anyway, nobody's giving anything to a Roma these days. We don't know how the tourists find out about these things so quick. Must be the staff in the hotels and cafés. I can imagine it:

"Watch those filthy Roma. They're capable of anything! And please don't encourage them onto the premises, Sir…Don't feel sorry for them. They get picked up at the end of the day in a BMW. I myself walk home in all weathers when I've finished here… Believe me, they've more gold chains under those rags than you could imagine. Shake a Roma and they jingle. That's what we say."

We've been on half rations for a week now and it might get less. We help one another but everybody's struggling. No one would want to rat on another Roma but people have to eat. Someone will break in time and whisper a name to the police. It will be Papa's name.

I found this report in a local newspaper. I've kept it folded in my waistband. My friend, Esma, told me what the words meant but the pictures scared me straight away. There are two police drawings of a Roma man and girl seen running away from the main square last week. They don't look very much like us. It *could* be me and Papa. But it could be just about any man or girl on the camp.

The newspaper also has a photo of the victim. An old photo. I'd have struggled to recognise him. In the photo, his face isn't so round as I remember it. He's also got more hair and isn't leering. And you can't get the smell from a photo. That sour stench of armpit and unwashed trousers.

Papa has a plan, though. He always does. It's not his idea really. It's what the Roma always do. Move on. He's going to get us out of Prague if the heat dies down enough. That's what he says: "Just let the heat die down enough."

He knows someone who can get us to the Slovak border, wherever that is. If we can slip into Slovakia overnight, the man will pick us up on the other side and take us to Bratislava. It's supposed to be a bit like here. Maybe not so many tourists. But enough Roma for us to disappear. Papa even knows people there. He's already used some gold to pay for it all. He's saved a bit to set us up at the other end.

I blame myself for what happened. How did I let him get near enough to corner me? I must have been tired. Not thinking. Or thinking about something else. Getting home. Food. It was the end of the day, just getting dusk. Still, I shouldn't have let him corner me in that alley off the square with Mama who-knows-where and Papa late coming to pick us up. I'd just gone to rest for a bit, out of the way and to let two municipal guards go past.

He must have been watching me and followed me down the alley. He called to me from behind:

"Hey! Don't run off. I won't hurt you."

He smiled a grimy smile:

"I just want to ask you something. And I've got something for you. Something nice. What's your name anyway?"

I moved the wrong way and got myself trapped in a doorway, with his great bulk between me and the way back to the main square. He put out his podgy hand, pushed back my head scarf and started stroking my hair with a crooked, blackened finger:

"There. What's the problem? We can be friends. I like the Roma. Good people. Friendly people. Friends. That's what we should be."

I played for time. Stood there, stock still, waiting for some idea to pop into my head. His hand went to his baggy trousers and disappeared. Still stroking, stroking away at my hair with one bent finger of his other hand.

Suddenly, he twisted sideways disturbed by something behind him. He moved to one side to reveal Papa, half his size, crouched with his blade in his right hand.

Papa couldn't get near him because of the man's great bulk and his outstretched arm, pushing back Papa's head. Papa stepped back, ducked below the out-stretched hand and tried to lunge forward with the knife but his leg slipped backwards on the damp cobbles. As Papa fell forward, the man struck him behind the ear. He hit the ground, right wrist first. The knife skidded across the cobbles. The man dropped onto Papa. His knees forced a groan from Papa's chest. He started to swing away at Papa's head with slow, heavy blows.

I picked up the knife, gripped it tightly in my hand and approached the man slowly from behind. All thoughts of me must have left his head. I planted both feet behind him, slightly to the right. I swung my right hand in a long, fast arc. I think the knife entered his neck just below his jaw. It didn't stop until my hand slapped against his fat jowls.

The pummelling stopped. He remained astride Papa for a while. There was a gurgling sound. He clawed at his neck. His chest heaved.

I stepped forward and pushed him as hard as I could with both hands. He fell sideways, freeing Papa. Papa stood up unsteadily and wiped some blood from his mouth and nose with a cloth. He steadied himself and gave the man a sharp kick in his side. There was no sound. I leaned over him and spat on his face. I couldn't stop myself.

Papa and I ran to the opening onto the main square and then slowed to a brisk walk. We did not speak.

« »

This new place is more than a hut. It's built of brick but the doors are missing. Probably chopped up for firewood last winter. Papa has put sacks over the doorway for the time being. Mama's already made it spotless inside but the smell outside is awful. There were a few of these two-room houses to choose from because no one wants them. They are next to a refuse tip, on the outskirts of Bratislava.

I miss my old hut back in Prague. Well, not so much the hut. I miss my friends more. And I have to learn new streets. The languages are pretty much the same though. That's the thing with Roma. We can make ourselves understood amongst our own folk anywhere. And we have a fresh start, my mistake in the Old Town Square in Prague now almost forgotten.

Papa doesn't moan about all the trouble we've had but I still blame myself. He says:

"These things happen. We are Gypsies. What can we do?"

"There's lots we can do," I reply one night. The next day, I burn my begging clothes.

Going Home

Some men are born to good luck: all they do or try to do comes right; all that falls to them is so much gain; all their geese are swans; all their cards are trumps. Toss them which way you will, they will always, like poor puss, alight upon their legs, and only move on so much the faster.

– Opening of "Hans in Luck" Jacob & Wilhelm Grimm

Hermannstadt, Romania, 1941

It's news to me but apparently I'm a *Volksdeutsch*, an ethnic German. When I get home from the meeting and tell my dad, his brothers, the neighbours, none of them have any idea about it either.

"So what's that mean, Hans? I suppose we have to pay taxes to Germany now, as well as here in Romania, do we?" my father asks.

"Don't know about that but it means I've got to go and fight. You're going to have to manage on the farm without me for a while. The SS man told us all today. Apparently, Hitler invented this *Volksdeutsch* word himself, just for us. We're supposed to be flattered, I think."

Dad tipped his hat back and scratched his forehead.

« »

Volksdeutsch? I've always thought we were just Swabians who happen to be in Transylvania, Romania. There are lots of us here. We've been here years, hundreds of years. I don't know exactly when we moved here from Germany. Why would I want to know? I wasn't very bookish at school. I don't like history. It just complicates everything. It doesn't help me plough or cut beet. I learn what I need to know from my parents and their friends and neighbours, listening in on long summer nights, when people gather outside as the air cools. Ach! We are here. We are doing fine. That's all I need to know.

We don't always get on with people in the other villages around us…the Romanians, the Gypsies and the like. But we rub along together most of the time. We're up before they are and still at it long after they've packed in for the day. So we prosper. We have tidy houses and farms, well-kept churches. Our full bellies and barns cause resentment but there are plenty of us and we keep an eye out for one another.

We speak, eat and worship in our German way. If you come to our village, the sights, the sounds, the smells… you'll think you're in Bavaria, Swabia or Saxony, where we came from all those years ago.

The Romanian government is trying to out-Nazi the Nazis. They're very cosy with Hitler anyway. They've given the SS a free hand with us *Volksdeutsch.* The SS tried to fill its battalions with volunteers at first. They thought we couldn't wait to join up and help the Führer's mission to free Eastern Europe of non-Germans. But after the hot-heads rushed off earlier this year, the volunteers dried up. I've never thought about Hitler's big idea much. It doesn't seem worth getting so worked up about. We're doing fine. My dad needs me on the farm.

Even so, I'll be conscripted in next week like it or not, along with a load of my mates. I've been summoned to join a Waffen SS Battalion being formed in Hermannstadt.

« »

"You lucky sod, Fassbinder! New boots. And they fit you. How did you manage that, you creep?"

These are Peter Müller's first words to me, Hans Fassbinder.

"No idea. I just took what I was given." I don't tell them I always seem to land on my feet, in this case in well-fitting combat boots.

"Lucky bastard! Stick near me when the lead starts flying. You'll be my lucky charm. Lucky Hans! You're my mate from now on," Müller replies. "OK?"

"OK!"

I don't know if I'll be able to keep the promise. I just want to shut him up. Stop him drawing attention to me amongst all these strangers.

There are a lot of guys called Hans joining the new Waffen SS Brigade in Hermannstadt today. Someone in the main square shouts "Hi Hans. Not seen you for a while" and six or seven guys turn around. Müller's sorting it out, though. He's giving out nick-names. Thanks to Müller, I've become "Lucky Hans" to distinguish me from "Big Hans", "Little Hans", "Hans the Red" and so on. I've no idea now what will happen to all the "Hanses". I hope my nick-name turns out to be true. I've no idea where we're going or what we'll be doing. It might be handy to stick near Müller. He seems to know what to do.

« »

I'm just twenty when I join up. I grow up quick, I can tell you. Very quick indeed. Over the next three years or so I see enough killing for a lifetime. Mainly Russians at first, but then, after we're whupped at Stalingrad, it's our turn to get it. It's not much fun advancing but sure as hell, it's better than retreating. That's one thing I've learned but it will not be much use back on the farm. If I ever get there, that is.

I eventually transfer to the Western Front. Big bit of luck! Müller has been right all along. In late '44, we both end up in a makeshift Panzer Division, the 17th SS Panzergrenadier Division Götz von Berlichingen. You can't forget a name like that. We're mainly *Volksdeutsch* from Silesia or Western Poland or guys from Romania like me, plus other odds and sods. We're supposed to be an elite unit but they take pretty much anybody now.

Only the hardcore Nazis amongst us still believe the war can be won. Some of the top brass have come for tomorrow's formal ceremony for the creation of the division. Someone says Himmler's here but I don't know what he looks like even if I see him.

What a mouthful..."17th SS Panzergrenadier Division Götz von Berlichingen". I have no idea who this Götz von Berlichingen guy was at first. We never learned anything about him back in my village school. An officer has explained it all today, in case any of the top brass asks us about it as they go up and down the lines inspecting us tomorrow, making sure we're spick and span before we march off into the mire.

Apparently Götz was some German knight from hundreds of years ago who got his hand blown off by a cannon ball. He had it replaced by an iron fist. That's our official insignia now. It won't be easy to be an iron fist when the Amis start hitting us day and night with a much bigger fist but we'll do our best.

According to the officer explaining it all to us, unlike me, *Götz von Wherever* wasn't especially lucky. Even after losing his hand, he managed to be on the wrong side in yet another battle. A messenger came to parlay with him as the battle entered its final phase. It went something like this:

"You position is hopeless, Sire. You are out-numbered many times over and completely surrounded. Surrender and we will give your men free passage. It is your only salvation."

That's how they talked in those days.

"Kiss my arse!" Götz replied.

He'd obviously missed the chivalry lesson at school.

We all think Götz's reply is funny when it's first explained to us. We respect the old guy. He had balls. It becomes our nickname with the Amis, the *Kiss my Arse Division.* But it gradually dawns on us that, most of all, the name is a reminder to us that surrender is not an option for Götz's boys. "Kiss my Arse" will be our response. Just before we get it shot off probably.

We are sent to disrupt allied beachheads in Normandy but it turns out to be hopeless. We are beaten back relentlessly, retreating across France to defend Metz, Saarbrucken, then finally we hole up in Bamberg.

So, here we are now, ready to re-group with other elite units in the old Nazi heartland, Bavaria. It's all coming to a head, nearly four years after getting those new boots and a nick-name in Hermannstadt. The boots wore out a while ago; the luck has lasted so far.

Bamberg, Southern Germany, April 1945

The Amis know exactly where we're holed up. Some of the civilians, our countrymen, must have told them. I don't blame them. They've had enough, too. Their beautiful town is being demolished in front of their eyes. They just want it to end. So we've had an artillery barrage for an hour or two, getting ever closer until the roof collapses and we are showered by dust and masonry where we lie.

When the barrage ends, it's Müller's turn to take a peek from the window to see what's happening. We lost our periscope weeks back. It was blown to bits along with the man carrying it. Müller just has to swallow hard and risk a look.

He puts his helmet on a broom handle and hoists it above a window-ledge to check for snipers. Nothing. He puts his helmet back on, crawls to the next window along and raises his head just enough to see over the ledge. He is shot through the right eye. He slumps back silently onto his haunches. He doesn't look surprised or anything. He just has a blank look in his remaining eye. Most of the damage is at the back of his head, where the bullet has exited. Something of Müller has splattered the shoulder of my tunic.

I don't know what to feel. I've been with Müller since joining up in Romania four years earlier. But the truth? I'm pleased it's not me sitting there on my haunches with the blank look. He always said I was a lucky so and so. Those were pretty much the first words he ever spoke to me. In many ways he was right. He always hoped my luck would rub off on him. He nick-named me "Lucky Hans" and then he became "Twin-Hans", although he isn't called Hans at all. It's just we've never seemed more than a few paces apart the whole war. But his luck finally runs out right here in Bamberg when it's his turn to take a peek out of the window.

I should now be in line to take the next peek but there'll be no more peeking for any of us.

We decided last night that we would surrender when the right moment comes, when we think the Amis won't mow us down on the spot. We have no officer left to threaten us with desertion. There's still Sigmund of course, the only one with the belief we could win the war because his fucking Führer says so. We just humour him most of the time. We've never been quite sure how he might react if we did run up the white flag. So we agreed secretly last night that someone would be behind him when the time came and would take him out if needs be.

Müller copping it is the clincher. Everybody liked him from the start. It convinces us the time is right. We look at one another and a nod is enough. So here in Bamberg, we finally forget our vows to Hitler and our defiant battalion motto. We are surrendering to the Amis.

And as for Sigmund? Not as stupid as we all thought! He must have guessed what was coming. He saved us the bother of shooting him in the back by doing the job himself in the middle of the night. Well, shot himself in the mouth actually. It's one of his spare vests that's tied to the broomstick as a white flag. It's spotless as befits a good SS man.

"Hands in the air!" the Yank shouts. "High in the air! Right up!" He prods Schmidt with the muzzle of his rifle. Schmidt's hands couldn't be much higher.

"Waffen fallen lassen! Hände hoch!" his officer adds in decent German, just to remove any doubt.

We have no doubt. We've had more than enough. We trudge out in weary single file behind Becker, leading with the white flag aloft. We stumble over the rubble in front the half-demolished house. Old Götz is probably turning in his grave at Germans doing all this arse-kissing. We don't care. We are just relieved it's over.

« »

We are herded into a temporary camp in a field outside Bamberg. We have no cover and it's cold at night. We are hungry, lousy, worn-out. At least no one's shooting at us and I'm alive. Even so, I am sore and low.

"Cheer up Hans! You're alive! Why so glum? Here, have a cigarette." It's Lothar, the Saarlander.

I ignore him.

"Hey man. You're not rotting and full of worms in some ditch in France. You're not on your way to a Russian labour camp where you'd die and nobody that cares about you would even know. Think on that. You're *Lucky Hans*. Act like him for God's sake!"

I'm sitting on the ground, alone amongst thousands of men in a field, most of them just happy that they're still in one piece. I have my head down:

"I keep thinking about Müller."

"You can't help Müller now. Or any of the others. Think about seeing your family again. We won't be prisoners forever. These Amis are ok. Better than the Ivans. Where is your family? Do you know?"

I don't answer. I don't want to talk to him, to anyone. I want to sit there and wallow in my black mood.

Lothar bends down to my level and looks me obliquely in the eye. I know he wants to help but I just stare ahead.

My relief at surviving has been replaced by an aching sense of all I've lost since leaving Romania. I've made it through. But to what? I have nobody to tell about it and nowhere to go home to. I curse the day I left the farm.

"It might have been better if I'd taken that bullet instead of Müller," I mumble.

I look up but Lothar has already disappeared back into the crowd.

« »

There are so many of us by now, the Americans just want us off their hands. They classify us by their own system. "Black" for hardcore Nazis and "white" for anti-Nazis. It's all a bit, well, German.

As a member of a Waffen SS regiment, I should be classified "black", and subject to tougher handling. But they know that I'm a *Volksdeutsch*, an ethnic German, and that some of us have never had much love for Nazism. I'm still quite young. That helps. Anyway, I don't care a damn what they do to me or where they send me. They realise I'm not putting on any act. So I'm classified "grey", non-political. I don't really care. They can do what they want with me.

It's a farce though. How can they judge? What do they know of what we've done? In truth, most of us have been different colours on different days, depending on how deep in mire we found ourselves and who was giving us orders...sometimes cruel, sometimes kind, sometimes just crawling scared into a hole and hoping it would all pass us by. "Grey" just about covers it.

I'm being sent to a camp in Yorkshire, wherever that is. Müller obviously isn't going with me. I'm not sure which of us has been lucky.

Do I want to go to this Yorkshire place? I've only one choice. Go or fake a break-out in front of a guard and take a bullet in the back. I can't decide. I'll trust to luck and toss a coin.

Buttfield Farm, Barmby, 1945

I've tossed my coin. I end up working on Buttfield Farm, on the edge of a village near Barnsley with two other PoWs. I would have been at home on a farm pretty much anywhere in Europe because I'm from farming stock. Though I feel at home on the farm, I am not at home in Yorkshire itself. Not at first at least. It might get better but it's so strange, this place.

I was used to the bitter Romanian winter but the wet cold of this sleeting land makes me miserable beyond measure. The cold seeps straight through my clothes like a freezing gas. The language is unintelligible. I know German and Romanian, bits of French and Russian. But this mumbling growl is like nothing I've ever heard.

Most of all, though, I miss my family. My brothers and sisters, nephews and nieces. My parents. I have no idea what has happened to them; where they are. Even whether they are alive or not. I have no idea what they know of my fate. The not-knowing wears me down. I feel an overwhelming unease, like a bile in my stomach.

I know from occasional letters from home received before the final collapse that things have got impossible for Germans in Romania. We are blamed for dragging Romania into the war on the wrong side. All the resentment about how we prospered over the years has spilled out. The last I heard from them, my parents were feeling besieged. They were thinking of setting off back to Germany with the retreating army in 1945, hoping that all those words of solidarity amongst the German peoples across Europe would mean something. It wouldn't really be *back* to Germany. That's wrong. Our families have not set foot in Germany for hundreds of years. It would be a foreign country, one that I already know is in chaos. In the last letter I got, my dad wasn't sure what to do.

So I don't know whether they ever made it back because the post dried up before he'd decided. I've had no Red Cross letter or parcel to set my heart racing. We get a camp newspaper, the *Wochenpost*. It gives us some idea of what's happening in Europe but only the big sweep and often months late. I found a really old copy with some news about Romania a while ago:

Wochenpost, December 1944
Soviet Forces Driving German Army out of Romania

Soviet forces are successfully driving remnants of the German 6th and 8th Armies and their fascist allies towards the Hungarian border. The advance is gathering pace and Romania should be free of Axis Forces within months.

Ethnic Germans, who have lived in Romania for centuries, are retreating in their thousands alongside Wehrmacht forces because of fear of reprisals from the majority Romanian population.

Update to follow in next week's Wochenpost.

I can't find a copy of the update. The uncertainty just makes me feel sick to the pit of my stomach.

So, I'm in no hurry to go home. I have no home; no-one and nowhere to return to. I still have images of my home in my head but I can't picture a future on the farm I left, only a past. I know that in my head is the only place that home still exists. That life has gone forever.

I'm so far away from anybody that really loves me. I desperately need just one person to see beyond the PoW uniform, beyond the fact that I'm one of thousands of aliens that might have done atrocious things. I need someone to notice me as a twenty-four year old without family or home. I need someone to look me in the eye and say: "Hello, Hans. How are you?… No, *really*. How are you?"

I need my biggest stroke of luck yet.

« »

Thank God I know farming and need little instruction. I just have to be nodded towards a job and I know what to do. Sometimes I do it in a way that impresses these dour folk, even if they don't say so. I know very well I'm lucky to be in Britain. These Yorkshire people don't waste words and are hard, it's true, but basically fair. If I'd been captured on the eastern front, I would have been long dead, shot in the back of the head by Russians or partisans or starved slowly along with the rest.

I have a lot of time to think things over. So much has happened. It seems a long way here in Yorkshire from those events in mainland Europe. I begin to think it's far enough away for me not to be forever condemned by what happened there. I can hope through the long winter evenings, lying tired in the bunk-house with the others. Hope I do. Hope is pretty much all I have for a while.

Everything that they are starting to hear about the camps means they should hate all Germans but these British can't be persuaded to hate in the abstract. That's our way, the way most Germans hate the Jews, the Slavs, the Gypsies, just for being Jews, Slavs and Gypsies, no matter what sort of human beings they actually are. Faced with a real live German, lonely, needy and more like them than they could have imagined, they can't maintain hate. By working hard, keeping my mouth shut, giving kindness and being grateful for any kindness received,

I start to show people who I really am…a sad, lonely and decent young man, caught up in events I can't fully understand, a long way from home, missing my family and with no idea what my future holds.

They gradually stop treating me as a Nazi PoW; stop calling me "Oy-you!" I thought that was a Yorkshire nick-name at first. Slowly, I become "Fassbinder", then just "Hans". They've begun to warm to me, their Hans. I start to get more perks: bits of food to take back to the camp that just happen to be left over from their meal; cast-off clothing; extra paid work. They now take time to correct my English. They even tease me gently, which in time I realise is a strange sign of affection amongst them. I am trusted with driving the tractor and with errands to the village. If any one of us is called into the farm house to get something, it's me.

I feel I'm being given a second chance; a chance to redeem myself for my part in the mess that my countrymen have created in our madness.

« »

It's now early 1947. I'm now the only one of three originals still making the daily trip to Buttfield Farm. To save on fuel and to make the most of the daylight, Mr Turner, my boss on the farm, suggests to the Officer in Charge at the camp that I be allowed to stay at Buttfield Farm Monday to Friday. He says he'll put a bed in one of the outbuildings and I can wash there. They'll supply me meals from the house, for which I'll have to pay a bit from my wages. The arrangement is agreed and I move into my outbuilding.

On one of my invitations into the kitchen I first meet Margaret. She's the pretty girl that comes from the pit village a mile away to help out in the kitchen and house. I've been asked in to pick up a sandwich and a flask of tea to take to Mr Turner, who's out in one of the further fields repairing some fencing. Margaret has wrapped the sandwich in grease-proof paper and it's lying on the table between us. As I reach to pick it up, she does the same. Our hands touch briefly. We both jerk our hands back, blushing and laughing nervously. It looks for a moment as if I'm going to put my hands up, in surrender again, but I quickly clasp them behind my back and wait for the next move.

"Please, excuse. Excuse me," I mumble.

She blushes some more.

Margaret hands me the sandwich, smiles, turns and hurries away to her other duties. I set off for the field in double-quick time, my heart thumping with the exertion of the walk across the ploughed field.

« »

I've recently started taking the farm dogs for walks in the summer evenings. I think of my distant homeland hills. I'm taking the sheepdog in hand a bit and teaching it a few useful tricks. I use German commands and so have to teach Mr Turner some German for him to make use of the tricks. He's not pleased when he's overheard by a neighbour talking to his dog in German:

"Bloody Hell, Frank! I thought we won the damned war!"

He pretends to be mad with me but he has become very tolerant of his willing, hard-working Hans.

Soon, I begin to stay over on the farm at weekends. My room in the outbuilding is a bit more welcoming by now, especially in summer. I have a light rigged up and can read to improve my English.

Margaret occasionally leaves a few meadow flowers in a jam jar on my window-sill. When I thank her for them, she blushes and says that Mrs Turner, the farmer's wife, told her to bring them but she doesn't look me in the eye and I know she's lying. It's all her idea.

"What's the name of these flowers in German?" she asks me.

"This one is *Mais chamille*...That one is *Kornblume*. Cornflower, you say in English."

"And that one?"

"That one is named after you...*Marguerite*!" I say.

"*Marguerite*," she repeats. "It sounds much nicer in German. *Marguerite*." She sets off towards the house, stops and half turns back: "I think we call some daisies *marguerite* in English now I think about it. You see, Hans. We're pretty much the same really."

For the rest of the summer, the flowers in the jam jar are always *marguerite*.

« »

I've started driving Mrs Turner and her teenage son and daughter to church each Sunday. "Evensong" they call it. A nice word, I think. Quite a German word in its way.

Mr Turner refuses to go to church any more.

"Where was your Almighty during all those goings-on in the concentration camps?" he asked his wife. "Seemed to be AWOL. So that's what I am on Sundays."

It's handy for him to have someone who can drive his family the couple of miles into the village and back for him. It gives him chance to have his weekly drink of whiskey without his wife's frown spoiling it. I sit in the car outside church, reading or just dozing till the service is over.

"What's your religion, Hans?" Mrs Turner asks on the return journey. "Back home, I mean."

"I don't know how you say in English…"

"Is it Catholic?" Patricia, the daughter, pipes up.

"No. Not Catholic. *Evangelisch* we say. I don't know the English for *evangelisch.*"

"Would you like to go to church, Hans? Do you miss going to church?" Mrs Turner asks.

I'm shocked. I hadn't been very religious before the war. Not compared with some. But our whole village went to church regularly anyway. It was always part of what kept us together. Lately, I've begun to hope and even to pray that someone or something will be looking out for my family for me. It comforts me to think that there might be some good at play after all the wickedness; to think that, choose how bad things had become, there is still a battle for right going on and it isn't lost yet.

I'm unsure: "Yes. Maybe. But not to embarrass anyone. I've never been in an English church before."

« »

On the following Sunday morning, Mrs Turner comes over to the outbuilding with a suit, a grey flannel shirt and a tie. She's got no shoes for me but I polish my work-boots until they're spotless every Sunday anyway.

"These are for you, Hans. To go to Church in tonight if you want to. I've asked the vicar. He says *evangelisch* is protestant. That's what we are. Well *Church of England* to be precise. He wasn't very keen on you attending at first, poor little man. Can't seem to decide anything by himself. I thought he might pray for a decision but he spoke to the parish leaders instead and it'll be ok. One of them lost a son, you see, in Normandy. We've lost quite a few boys from the village. It's still a bit raw for some here. But, anyway, if we don't start to forgive, we'll never move on from the blooming war. He wants you to sit at the back at first. Billy will sit with you and help you with the responses. Do you want to go?"

She peers into my eyes but I give nothing away. It's a big step.

"Think about it, Hans. Just think about it."

She puts the clothes on my bed and leaves.

I do think about it. All day, fretting away.

At half past four, I give my work-boots another polish and put on Mr Turner's old suit. It will go round me twice but it's better than the jacket with "PoW" on the back. I'm nervous as hell but excited too.

We are a bit late setting off as Mrs Turner insists on re-doing my tie, in the Church of England style I think.

"This is how we do it, Hans. You're in England now."

I've done it the only way I know how, the Waffen SS way. It might get me thrown out of church. I fear she's going to spit on her hand and smooth down my hair but thankfully she doesn't.

My heart pounds as I enter the church. It is full when we get there. Every head turns and every eye bores into me as Billy ushers me to a pew at the back. I seem to know many of the hymn tunes and some of the responses. With Billy's help, we make it through with *Amen* and *Thanks be to God* more or less in the right places.

I love it. The booming organ, the deep, mumbled responses from these solid people, restrained even in their religion. I think of all the people across Europe, over all the miles to Hermannstadt, singing, praying, and trying to work out what to do with their lives. I imagine my parents in a church somewhere at that very moment, kneeling and praying for me. My eyes fill with tears, but happy tears. For the first time since I left our little village, I feel connected to them.

As I file out last, with Billy alongside me, the little vicar gives me a broad smile, happy no doubt that everything has passed without incident.

"Nice to see you, Hans. Hope to see you again."

I mumble my thanks.

The vicar's words run round my head all the way home and come back to me in the fields all week:

"Nice to see you, Hans."

« »

I've been desperate to find a way of thanking people for accepting me at the church, where Billy and I now sit immediately behind Mrs Turner and Patricia. I still get stern looks from some, but most people now greet me with at least a nod and the glimmer of a smile. It's enough.

I've been busy in the run-up to harvest, working most days when it's fine and taking days off or catching up on odd-jobs when it isn't. In the week before Harvest Festival, I knock on the kitchen door and fidget from foot to foot waiting for it to open. When Mrs Turner comes to the door, I blurt out that I've made something for the harvest display, but "only if it's good enough." I fear it will be too late to include it this year but I know Mrs Turner has something to do with the festival. She might find somewhere to slot it in. I put the old hessian sack containing the gift just inside the door, turn tail and go back the outbuilding before she can look at it.

« »

As we enter the church on the night of the harvest festival, I feel transported back to my home village. The harvest decorations are not as colourful as ours are. They can't be. This produce hasn't been soaked in sun like our crops. There are more browns and greys here. No bright-red peppers. But the profusion is just as great and the humble thanks for another harvest is just as heartfelt.

Inside the entrance, the christening font is full to the brim with flowers; sunflowers, geraniums, delphiniums, yellow rudbeckia. Its base is encircled in fruit: apples, plums, red, purple and black berries. The end of each pew is decorated with a corn dolly of some sort... crosses, sheaves, fish. The top of the pulpit is bordered with more autumn flowers, mixed with greenery from the hedgerows.

The altar is laden with vegetables of every sort, parsnips, potatoes, leeks, radishes, onions. Big baking apples have been cored and candles inserted into them. At the centre of the altar lies a massive piece of bread in the form of a sheaf of corn. Behind it rises the altar crucifix.

As I kneel to pray, I spot my own piece. It is in pride of place, centrally in front of the altar.

Some weeks ago, I'd found a large off-cut from an oak beam lying around in the barn and had asked Mr Turner for it.

"Aye. You can have it lad if you can make 'owt of it. It might stop you mooning over Margaret if you've something to occupy your mind."

I didn't understand the bit about Margaret. I was scared to ask what he meant.

I took my chance with the wood. A lot of us at home had whiled away the long winters back home carving. What time I had, I gave to the carving. I made a triangular base from floor-boarding. To decorate the front of the base, I carved a frieze from a band of oak that I'd sheared off the main block. It comprised English fruit and vegetables.

Then, leaning inwards from the two front corners of the base, I'd fixed two identical sheaves of corn, about a yard each in length and carved from the lovely, mellow English oak. These joined at a point above the centre of the base, as if leaning together in the field.

Mrs Turner had filled the base with the most colourful fruit available so that they were framed by the two sheaves. She'd used all the English varieties of apple, plums, the ripest berries, chestnuts, tomatoes...anything with a bit of colour. She'd polished the apples and nuts so they gleamed in the light from the candles.

As I look at my work, there as the centre-piece of the decorations in this English church, my eyes brim yet again. I mumble my prayers and then sit back, looking down to avoid eye-contact until my eyes dry.

« »

Margaret and I are now snatching quick conversations under the eye of most of the villagers after Evensong. She, too, has started attending church and sits with Mrs Turner and Patricia directly in front of me and Billy. I can look directly at her hair and the back of her neck. I get lost in thought as I fix my gaze on her neck. I keep missing responses. Billy digs me in the ribs and smirks:

"Now, now, Hans. Mind on the job!"

I've also developed the habit of starting jobs just before lunch so that Margaret has to bring my lunch out to wherever I'm working after they've all finished. It's not as tasty eaten cold but it's made all the nicer for having Margaret with me while I eat it. She waits for me to finish so that she can take the plate back but that doesn't really make sense. I could do that myself but I'm glad of the company. Well, I'm glad of her company.

Through that summer, we talk about nothing and we fall in love.

« »

Margaret gives me ever more cause to believe that I might have a better life here in England, despite the dreadful weather and the soggy food. With her help, I work at being accepted for what I know I am, an honest, decent man who needs and wants just the same as everyone else ...a family, with Margaret at its centre, work, food, peace and safety. This becomes our mission, Margaret's and mine.

We secretly plan the future, not daring at first to speak of it with anyone. It's a bit like the snakes and ladders game we played back at the camp. At first, there seem to be more snakes in the game than there are ladders. Further revelations from the camps; someone local who's been badly wounded but has survived for a while might die; a prominent Nazi is arrested and his misdeeds exposed to the world – all these developments make our plans seem hopeless.

But things also happen to encourage Margaret and me to think we might just have a future together in England. These ladders usually appear completely out of the blue.

One lunch-time in August 1947, Margaret runs over to my door when I return from the fields:

"Hans! Hans! Some news from the paper. I've cut it out for you. It's good news!"

She's breathless. She thrusts the clipping into my hand. I can make out the headline:

PoW marries English Woman:
Local Public Opinion Mixed.

I don't know some of the words in the report so she snatches it back and reads it for me, missing out bits I don't understand:

"Heinz Felbrich, a German PoW, and his new wife June (nee Tull) were celebrating quietly yesterday after their marriage made history. Heinz is the first German PoW to wed an English woman since such marriages were legalised last month.

There has been considerable hostility to the marriage in Southampton, where the couple live, separately for the time being. There are reports of Miss Tull (19) having been spat at in the street and being called "Traitor Bride!" after news of the plans for the wedding became public. Miss Tull faced opposition even within her own family although her mother is supportive. Opposition has been strongest from those who lost relatives in the war.

Wedding celebrations were short-lived. Herr Felbrich was required to return to his PoW camp at dusk under the terms of his confinement. It is not known when the couple will be able to set up home together.

"If they managed it, so can we! We just need to bide our time."

I look puzzled.

"You know. Be patient. Wait until the time is right."

We do bide our time until eventually we feel brave enough to share our hopes with others, first with Margaret's best friend, then her family, finally with Mrs Turner. No one beyond that group says anything openly, but we know that others in the village are suspicious from the looks we get.

« »

One day, Mr Turner sends word with Billy for me to go see him in the kitchen. I go in, cap in hand, and stand to one side of the massive table where he sits, his great fists clasped before him. He can't look me in the eye. Mrs Turner is standing in the background tight-lipped with anger. I guess I've done something wrong. Mr Turner is embarrassed. I get the feeling they've had a row about something. He struggles for the words:

"Hans. Jim Atkins has been to see me, Margaret's dad." He shuffles in his chair. "It's got to stop, lad. Got to stop."

I look from him to Mrs Turner. She glowers at her husband. I look back, still silent.

"Jim…Mr Atkins that is…thinks you and Margaret have got, well, too close. You are just about courting and it's not on. Folk are talking. Jim's getting it in the neck from people in the village. People who lost loved ones in the war. It's all a bit tense with Remembrance Day coming up. It's just too soon, lad. Anyway, it's got to stop. If it doesn't, Jim'll stop Margaret working here. Either that, or you'll have to go. One or t'other."

I can't assemble the words to protest. Margaret and me…it has just happened. We like one another's company. I make her laugh and she makes me feel like a normal young man again. What's wrong with that?

These thoughts never leave my head. All I can do is splutter:

"But that's not, how you say …"

"No good arguing, lad. I like you. We all like you. You're a good worker and a decent chap. We trust you. But we have to live here when you've gone back and we have to think about folk we've known all our lives…It's got to stop."

The chair grates on the stone floor as he pushes it abruptly back. He stands up, turns sharply and leaves. His wife follows him. I turn and go to my outbuilding, pack my things and leave for the five mile trek to the camp.

It's over.

« »

I spend about two weeks back at the camp waiting for a decision about what happens to me next. I am hurt and confused. I don't want to go back to…where? Romania? Germany? Where in Germany? Where is my family…my home?

Equally, I can't stay here, taunted by the life I might have had. It would be too much to bear. I spend long, long days with nothing to do but think about what I've lost since that cursed day I left Hermannstadt.

On the afternoon of the third Sunday after leaving the farm, I'm lying on my bed in the room I share with seven others, dozing and smoking and tossing and turning, trying to avoid conversation with my camp-mates.

Another prisoner comes rushing in:

"Fassbinder. You've got visitors. Not one woman. Two! What have you got that we haven't. I've seen you in the showers. Nothing special. Get yourself down to the office, before they change their mind and ask to see me instead."

It's Mrs Turner and Margaret. Margaret smiles weakly as I come in. I stand to attention in front of the Officer in Charge.

"At ease, Fassbinder…Mrs Turner, Miss Atkins and I have been discussing your…your situation. At the farm, that is. There's been something of a change of mind. Mr Turner has decided you can have your old job back. In fact he's prepared to keep you on until such time as you're granted leave to stay, when he's prepared to offer you regular employment on the same basis as anybody else resident in this country."

He lights a cigarette.

"Do you understand what I'm saying, Fassbinder? I know you've been unsettled recently and may need time to think about all this. You can have a fortnight to make a final decision about repatriation but that needn't stop you returning to Buttfield Farm on Monday."

It's a lot to take in. But there's more.

"There have been other matters discussed, too. Personal matters." He becomes brusque: "That's not for me to share though. That's for Miss Atkins. For propriety's sake, Mrs Turner will stay with you whilst Margaret tells you about all that. I'm going to leave you three together now."

He stands to leave but pauses briefly: "So. A fortnight, Fassbinder. Decide and let me know. Sooner if you can."

As soon as he's gone, Margaret begins to squirm in her chair.

"Go on Margaret. Get on with it. It's good news so get a move on," Mrs Turner prompts.

"It's good news in a way. If Hans sees it that way, that is," she whispers without looking at me. "It's my Dad, Hans. He's changed his mind. He's ok about us courting."

She looks up at me for a reaction.

I can hardly believe it. I've never known these

Yorkshire people to change their minds in all my time there. They're not a mind-changing people.

"Why? What do I have to do?"

"You don't have to do anything. He's always liked you, you know. Deep down. He thinks you are, well, ok. That's pretty good for my Dad, believe me. He finally said 'It grieves me to say it but he's better than some of these cocky buggers of ours coming back the conquering heroes and lording it over the rest of us!' "

She looks down at her feet: "Anyway, I've been so miserable. We've been arguing all the time over it at home. I finally told him that I would be twenty-one soon and then I'd go to Germany and find you and marry you over there. And stay. We'd have his grandchildren but he'd never see them. I told him I'd started making some enquiries about it. He wouldn't be able to do anything to stop me. He knew I'd do it as well. Then, even Mum turned against him."

She looks at Mrs Turner for reassurance. Mrs Turner just maintains her smile and Margaret continues:

"But what finally swung it was Mrs Sutcliffe, you know, the lady who runs our village shop. She and her husband lost their only son in a bombing raid over Germany. He was a pilot in a Lancaster. Robert had been some sort of engineer at the pit before he joined up. Dad has always worried most about what the families that have lost someone think of me carrying on with a German. Mrs Sutcliffe heard about how upset I've been. Anyway, she came to see Dad and told him he was wrong.

Came straight out with it, right there in his own front-room. Her nightmare had always been of Robert falling injured and in pain amongst those Nazis. She knew they'd hate him. They'd do awful things to him. Her way of coping was to pray that if he fell from the sky injured, someone decent would find him and treat him like a son. She thought there must be a few decent people left in Germany."

She pauses.

"Of course, Robert did fall from the sky. But he was dead. So for her, one nightmare replaced another. She was inconsolable… You know, Hans…Really, really upset."

I screw up my eyes. I can't work out what this means for me.

Margaret continues:

"But Mrs Sutcliffe said that in time, she began to feel that her prayers hadn't been wasted after all. They hadn't helped her son, but they could help someone else's. You are a fine boy, a credit to someone, she knows that. 'He's someone's son,' she said. 'Someone's missing him'."

"Her final words were: 'You couldn't do your bit at the front for the war. Do your bit for the peace, Jim. Treat him fairly; treat him like a son'."

"With that, she stood up, turned and left for home. We were speechless. The next day, Dad told me to get my coat because we were going to Buttfield Farm."

« »

Margaret and I marry six months later. I stay at the farm a couple of years after that. But with a baby on the way, I need more money than Mr Turner can pay. So I get a job at the pit in the village that Margaret grew up in and we move into a terraced house there. Eventually, our son is born, with a mop of black hair, my black hair.

Barnsley, Christmas 1958

Sometimes, I have to concentrate hard to remember where I am on this earth. Like today. It could be anywhere. The exertion of the trek up the steep hill through thick snow has left me a bit light-headed. And the snow disguises all the familiar landmarks.

I lean against a tree on the edge of the wood and light a cigarette. I wait for the two boys to catch up with me. One is dark-haired, the other blond. They trudge up the hill, leaning into the slope, eyes down, jabbering away as usual. It's always too fast for me to understand even though I've lived and worked in England for more than a decade now.

The dark-haired boy is my son, Michael. That's my dark hair he has. Not all Germans are blond-haired and blue-eyed, as you English think. The blond-haired boy, Paul, is his best mate. If you'd had to pick the German's son, you'd have picked Paul. You'd have been wrong. Things are not always what they seem.

We have just about the strangest surname in the village, Michael, Margaret and I: Fassbinder. I am the only

German around here but there are Czechs, Poles and a few other odds and sods. After a bit of unpleasantness, my name gradually turned from Hans to John. Down the pit we're all alike. The men band together against everybody else...deputies, managers, toffs; the rest of the world really. Differences are forgotten in the dust and heat and half-light. They have pretty much forgotten that I'm German.

We are out for a walk. It's a few days to Christmas 1958, my 13th in England. The coal mine where I work is shut down for the festive season. We're marking time to the big day and this morning, we've been banished from home.

"For Heaven's sake, get from under my feet!" she shouted. "If you want a Christmas dinner on Thursday, you need to let me get on."

It's all getting to Margaret a bit. She wants Christmas Day to be so perfect for us. It's a lot of work and I'm not much use around the house or kitchen. Mince pies? A mystery to me. Stuffing? Strange idea! Tastes no better than what was in the bird originally. And trifle? A bit like sweet baby-sick. Not for me, thanks. I know about goose, carp, stollen. But not this stuff. So much of the work falls to her, I'm afraid.

I needed no second invitation to get outside into the fresh air. After all, I grew up on a farm, over a thousand miles away across Europe. I was always used to being out in the open. I usually had my head down in the fields, it's true, but if I looked up while easing my back for a moment, I saw only gently rolling, wooded hills.

I never moan about it to anyone here because I'm "bloody lucky", as I've been told all my life, but the hardest thing I've had to get used to is working down the mine. When I'm hacking away at the coalface, I could just as well be digging a field back home. But when I look up from my work now, all I see is a low ceiling of rock, boxing me in like an oversize coffin lid. It took some getting used to I can tell you but I do it for my family. I've done worse things in my time.

So I was off willingly this morning. The two boys needed a bit more persuasion. They were playing Subbuteo in front of the coal fire but the promise of a Wagon Wheel from Sutcliffe's shop got them going.

It's eerily quiet up here on top of the hill. Nothing much is moving in the valley below. The covering of snow makes everything neater and tidier and prettier, like a scene on these Christmas cards people give one another. The great wheels on the pit head-gear are still. The coal wagons are under snow in the sidings. The smoke from the rows of cottages drifts slowly up to a clear blue sky. Everyone is busy indoors, baking, putting decorations up, wrapping presents and hiding them away. If I shut everything else out of my mind, the narrow valley below could even be my faraway hills.

When it's not disguised under snow, this village is not much to look at. We'd call it a *Kaff* in German. A "dump" you would say. But it has woods all around it and nobody's been taken out and shot in the back of the head in my time here. If I get a bit down in the dumps, thinking about what's happened, Margaret always tells me "home is where the heart is." She's right, as ever. My heart's here now. With her, with our son, with my in-laws. I have truly found more than I lost. Much more. I have Margaret. I have my son, Michael. Peace. Food on the table. Work. My comrades at the pit. My in-laws do treat me like a son, just as Mrs Sutcliffe said they should.

I crouch down to take the weight off my legs and look to see how long the boys will be. The branches on the trees behind me are heavy with snow, great lumps of which slither to ground occasionally as the winter sun takes effect. Such sudden noise doesn't make me jump like it would have done immediately after the war.

So now you know as much as me. You may even understand it a bit better than I do. I know *what* happened. I was there through it all. But I still haven't worked out *why* it happened. Why I, a German, grew up on a farm in Romania, then fought my way across Europe? Why it was Müller's turn to risk a peek through the broken window, not mine? Why I left all those other farm boys in the ditches and fields of Europe while I shuffled on to meet Margaret on a farm in the middle of nowhere? And why a woman I hardly knew spoke up for me against her own people? My head spins with it all and I still have to pinch myself to be sure it's all true. But it is, thank God! Not for what happened but that I've come through it.

If you know why it all happened as it did, you're much cleverer than me. But please don't talk to me about fate or destiny or faith or whatever other word you want to use. That sounds too much like a plan. Or a big book somewhere with it all written down in nice neat columns. What's going to happen to every human in the whole world. A chapter for the Jews, one for the Poles, one for the Czechs and Germans and so on. I can't believe that. There was no plan. Perhaps there is no "why?" either. You've no idea what will happen at the start of things. You take that first step, willingly or prodded forward from behind, but you don't know where it will lead you. In some ways that's a good thing.

I look down towards the boys, who've stopped to try to dislodge snow from the trees with a few well-aimed snowballs. I don't hurry them. It gives Margaret more time.

I read Michael my favourite fairy tale, *Hans in Luck*, before bed last night. He's been excited with Christmas coming and a story helps him settle. He thinks fairy tales are much too childish for him now and he's probably right. I read them anyway, like my Dad did to us back on the farm. We Germans love our fairy tales and *Hans in Luck* was always my favourite. Michael fell asleep quickly but I stayed beside his bed reading the story silently to its end, just for me.

Sometimes I feel a bit like Hans in the fairy story. You may not know how it goes. Hans sets off on a long journey home after many years away. He makes it home to his old mother, after lots of scrapes and adventures. I like the way that, whatever happens to him, Hans makes something positive from it. And I like the way it all turns out fine in the end, a bit like it's done for me. It makes me smile to myself. It makes me think about what I've lost but also what I've found. Different language; different place; different food; different work...but a family just the same. My family now.

Of course *Hans in Luck* is only a story; only one part of his life. He's still a young man when it ends. Anything could still happen to him. Does he marry? Have kids? Prosper? Live long and die peacefully in his bed? We only know part of his story. I'd love to know the rest. It's not really over, is it? It's never over.

I've not made it home to my mother but at least I've found another home. Like Hans, I got lucky. I got a second chance and took it. Did I deserve it over the millions killed in the gas chambers, in the ditches, back streets and cellars across Europe? Probably not. It's not for me to say. All I can do is make the best of the chance I've got.

But, like the Hans in the story, I feel blessed. I dig coal for a living but I've found gold in the end.

The two boys are nearing me now, blowing a bit as they reach the brow of the hill, walking in single file in my great big snow prints.

"Can we go back yet? We're puffed out!"

"No. Sorry boys. No going back."

I put my arm around Michael's shoulder to encourage him along but he shrugs it off. His mate's there after all.

We trudge on into unmarked snow.

Epilogue

Barnsley Chronicle 6th March 1959

Fatal Accident at Woolley Colliery
A fatal accident occurred at Woolley Colliery on Monday this week. The Chronicle understands that Hans Fassbinder, a face-worker, was crushed by a fall of rock whilst working on the Parkgate seam. Mr Fassbinder received first aid at the scene but was pronounced dead in the colliery medical room. No one else was injured in the accident. As required by the Mines and Quarries Act, Mr Fassbinder's death has been reported to the District Safety Board. There will be an Inquest at a date to be determined. No further details were available as the Chronicle went to press.

Widow's Weeds

I am the only one who knows why a sun-bleached rabbit's skull has pride of place on my mantelpiece. Slightly behind it is a framed photograph of my late husband, striding out to open the batting for our village team as he'd done, man and boy, for thirty five years until that fateful day. "Boy and boy", that should be. Cricketers never really grow up.

In the photograph, he's totally focussed on the half century he didn't score. He's dressed immaculately, from the top of his helmeted head to the toe of his brand new white boots. I keep his photo up there for appearances but when the time's right it'll go in the bin.

He'd bought the new boots on one of our rare shopping trips together. I'd had to sit there while he tried on endless pairs of almost identical boots. Of course, he bought the dearest. He always confused "be the best" with "buy the best". He opted for the ones with flashy stripes and interchangeable studs so he could select exactly the right stud for the conditions. He was really keen on that idea. Yawn!

Having made me sit through an hour of this, he had the gall to give me the hurry-up when I paused to look at a pair of lovely little stud earrings in a jewellers shop nearby. He shuffled impatiently from foot to foot and mumbled a mournful:"They're bloody dear. There's nothing to them."

He'll pay, I thought. Not for the earrings obviously but he'll pay for something, somehow.

The coroner said that the boots were the main factor in the accident. More than half the studs were missing apparently. They had been loose and were found at all the points on the ground where he'd stood earlier. Fancy that! First time on, too.

It had rained earlier in the week and the turf in the outfield was still greasy on the Saturday of the match. Apparently, when he ran to take the catch and turned one foot in the hole a rabbit had dug the night before, the new boots failed to give any grip. He plummeted forward, breaking his neck as he drove his head into the ground.

I couldn't have foreseen this, obviously. Had I intended it? You judge. It depends what you mean by "intend." I'd probably only meant to irritate him a bit. Have him slip and slide around and, with a bit of luck, end up on his backside at some point. But it's an ill-wind as they say…

Yes, a real pity for him. But not for me. I was about to leave him anyway after thirty years of sitting home alone every summer Saturday afternoon. Well, he thought I was home alone. Sometimes I was home and sometimes I was alone and occasionally I was both together. His accident saved a lot of bother. It also left me nicely set up, what with insurance pay-outs, an out-of-court settlement from the boot company and the like.

I felt obliged to go to the memorial game that his mates organised for him at the end of the season. I put on a show of restrained grief, saying little because I had nothing to say to these pot-bellied adolescents. I think they interpreted my reticence as grief, not the boredom it was. But I simply had to get away from all the cricket chatter in the pavilion when they began to recount his greatest performances. Not that I personally recall many of those in any aspect of his life. Anyway, this talk was tedious beyond endurance and of course, I'd heard it all before, from him.

So I took a slow turn around the ground, alone in my widow's weeds. I'm sure they were all impressed by the black silhouette, inching its way around the far boundary. That's where I spotted the rabbit skull, there where the cricket ground borders a farmer's field. I couldn't know whether it was *the* rabbit, my fairy god-rabbit, the one that had changed my life forever. No matter. It was probably at least related.

The rabbit had turned me into a proper cricket widow after years of rehearsal. The skull deserves pride of place in my front room. No one else knows why. No one has ever asked.

"What was that? Yes, Darling! Of course I'll have a martini. The sun's over the yardarm," I shout through to the kitchen.

One Day as a Lion

Toul, France.

The two women were finally about to visit the man they hadn't seen for fifteen years. They had both loved him in different ways, one as a sister, the other as his fiancé.

Much had delayed this visit to France. His ex-fiancé, now thirty, had initially not wanted to visit her first love out of loyalty to her second. But the marriage she entered whilst still confused and hurt at his leaving had not lasted long. She was now free to visit him. And what had gotten in the way for the man's younger sister? Well, life had gotten in the way...bringing up children and getting together enough money to travel to France. Both had also needed time to work through their hurt at him for leaving them so abruptly for reasons they never fully understood.

It had been a long, arduous journey, by bus, train, night ferry and then the same again in France, the second half of the trip conducted in their little bit of French but they'd managed it. It had been inevitable. They were now finally in the town of Toul, where he had been exiled for a decade with no visit from home.

The women had spent the day before the meeting preparing. They were nervous enough at being abroad for the first time. They'd needed time to clear their thoughts for the visit.

They were so near to him now, but these surroundings didn't seem to have anything remotely to do with the young man they remembered from their Yorkshire village. It was not the destination they would have imagined for him years ago.

The day of the visit dawned bright and clear. They picked at their breakfast. The strong coffee had made them both queasy and they'd managed only a few sips each. They were to meet a short distance outside the town. They arrived much quicker than they'd expected. They nervously smoothed the creases from their skirts after their short taxi ride, patted their hair into position and turned away from the road towards their designated meeting place.

September 1939, a coal mine in South Yorkshire

'I am. I'm going to fly for the RAF. It will definitely happen.'

Robert stated this over the clatter of the machinery. He stared into the distance, ignoring the conveyor-belt of coal passing before the line of grimy young men. He was not sharing this news with them. Rather he was telling himself. The firmer he said it, the more certain it was to happen.

"Yeah. And pigs will fly! In RAF uniforms as well."

His workmates were all smirking. Bloody ideas above his station, he had! People like that got taken down a peg or two. Your life was mapped out for you. You followed your dad down the path from village to coal mine. When your dad stopped making the trip, you kept going, followed by your own son.

"Wait and see," he said, too quietly to be heard over the din.

Robert, 17, was a trainee mining engineer when war broke out. Coal mining was a job for life but in Robert's mind it was temporary. Mining was a reserved occupation in this war so his workmates were in no hurry to join up. But Robert marched to a different drum. He had relatives in Canada who, years earlier, had sent him comics featuring Luke Star, Sky Ranger, an aviator-hero who used his plane to save mankind from assorted villains. Luke Star ignited a flame in young Robert that burned still. Six years on, he knew exactly what he wanted to do with his life. He wanted to fly and be a hero. He *would* fly. He just had to work out how.

Yesterday, Robert had seen a notice in the paper seeking young men keen to fly in the RAF. It was the message he'd longed for. This new war was the *how*.

« »

Robert's dad, a cricket fanatic, was jealous when he heard that his son was going to Lord's, now an RAF recruitment centre. He and his wife were not pleased about the purpose of the visit, however. His dad couldn't understand why Robert wanted to go and get himself into the cockpit of a plane and fly into the German guns? He had personally seen enough slaughter in the Great War. He didn't want that for his son.

Robert wasn't interested in cricket. He would never willingly have gone through the gates of Lords had it not been requisitioned by the RAF. He'd have to report back to his father on how the ground looked and whether it would be ready for the cricket that would resume when this war ended.

Robert was nervous as he reported for various tests as to his suitability for an aircrew role, perhaps even as a pilot. He was confident in himself though. He knew his desire was strong. He believed in his own ability and good nerves. He learned quickly. He'd been really good at technical stuff. He coped with noise and dust and cramped conditions. He went into dangerous places down the pit. Coal face; cockpit…what's the difference? He'd be OK. He was as good as any of them.

His parents had half-hoped the interview board might find something minor wrong with him. Not enough to blight his life but just enough to restrict him to tinkering with the planes on the ground. He could wave them off to Germany and then patch them up on their return.

It was no surprise to Robert but was a disappointment to his Mum and Dad that he passed his interview with ease. He compounded this in his father's eyes by forgetting to assess the state of the Lord's wicket before he left.

« »

Robert went on Initial Training for three months of PE, drill and classroom work that would gradually identify him for a specific aircrew role. His life was now moving in the direction he'd dreamed of since reading his first Luke Star adventure.

Two years of training inched him nearer to his goal. He simply kept going, working, memorising, with all the concentration he could muster, until he finally got his wings. He was commissioned as a Pilot Officer, a sign that he had done well in his training.

Despite their immense pride, his father's shoulders shrank a bit; his mother went quiet.

« »

Crewing-up was the process of creating the seven-man team that would live and possibly die together in one of the RAF bombers. It was a deceptively casual affair. Airmen of every specialty were simply put together in a big hangar where they selected themselves into crews by no rules other than that they had to have one man of every role.

The ability of the pilot was the most serious consideration. They were now within weeks of their first mission. Two years earlier, their colleagues had been guys to joke and drink beer with. Now they were being evaluated, not for their skill at darts or their chat-up lines but whether they could plot their course home in cloud and smoke or keep their nerve and shoot straight? Airmen had little to help them decide…just what they knew from training and instinct. In the end, they trusted to luck. Trusting to luck was good preparation for what was ahead.

Robert stood tall in the middle of the hangar, trying to look unconcerned that he was still alone. He felt a tap on the shoulder, turned and looked down at a wiry man with an unlit Park Drive hanging from one corner of his mouth.

"Are you any bloody good then, Guv?" asked the smaller man, in the first cockney accent Robert had ever heard.

"Not crashed yet!" replied Robert, his northern vowels not quite as flat now as when he started his training over two years earlier.

"Good enough for me! I finished second-top in gunner training. All that practice robbing banks before the war. Jimmy Johnson's the name. Minner to me mates. Don't ask why. Am I in?"

"I suppose so," said Robert. "Just two of us so far. Plenty of room still."

That wasn't true for long. Momentum built. Unattached men thought others must know something they didn't and gravitated towards nearly complete crews. Robert quickly acquired Ken, a Scottish navigator, who recommended Alex, a bomb aimer. Aidan had been apprenticed at Rolls Royce, recommendation enough for the role of Flight Engineer. Stuart Wainwright, another Yorkshireman, became their Wireless Operator. Newcastle-born Geoffrey Grigson filled the slot as Mid-gunner. The crew was complete.

The conversations through which they would blend into a proper crew began. Minner helped: "Bloody 'ell! I think you should take some elocution lessons Stuart, mate. How the 'ell are we going to understand a Yorkshire wireless operator?"

Now oblivious to the other crews, a buzz developed around them as they got to know one another. They were entering their own little world of seven. Robert was quietly pleased. Although he still hardly knew these men, he had a good feeling. It would be alright.

« »

Leave back home in Yorkshire was bitter-sweet for everyone involved. It was always longed for. Crew banter fed on it beforehand and on the gilded versions of events afterwards.

It was great to see Marjorie and his family; to wallow in their love and respect and the warmth from all in the village. But in truth, Robert often felt nearly as churned-up when launching into a home-leave as when setting off for Germany. He didn't know why. Was it separation from his crew? Fear of returning to ops after time-off? Seeing his parents' worry?

Robert would sit by the fire that blazed winter and summer and stretch his long legs out before him. He held court as a succession of neighbours and relatives just happened to be passing. The kettle was permanently simmering away on the fire-side. They supped their tea from big white mugs. They came to look at his uniform, with the insignia that showed that he was special, even amongst the bravest.

At home, he tried to relax and sleep his old, youthful sleep. But he couldn't. He could never quite exclude his other life. To let go of it was to lose control and in just a few days time, he would need to be back in total control. He dreaded being caught out, unprepared, slow to react. So, even at home, even in the pub with his mates, even in the quiet moments with Marjorie, he could not relax completely.

He felt responsible for his family at home, just as he did for his crew. He himself knew that he was only at risk when up in the sky; his family, however, worried about him constantly because they never knew whether he was tucked up in bed or whether some German fighter pilot had him in his sights at that very moment. It was brief, intense terror for him but a draining, interminable worry for them.

On leave there would also be the inevitable debate about why? Why he'd volunteered? Why Bomber Command? Why active operations? Why a pilot, the last one to bail out?

Robert smiled. He was ready for it. He'd heard it for three years by now.

"Somebody has to do it. You can't stand back and leave it to others, Mum."

She was not convinced. Lots of men were doing just that.

"…and we can't let the Germans take over everywhere. They've had their own way too long. What would life be like if they came over here?"

"Yes, but couldn't you do something else? Something with your technical training?" his mother would ask, hopefully. "Surely they need people to repair these planes when they come back with holes in them and engines dropping off …"

"…but they need pilots more, mother. And just think of the career I can have after the war. Flying, anywhere in the world! Anywhere they'll need pilots."

In truth, the career argument was irrelevant. Robert could not think so far ahead. He coped with the risks by shortening his horizons. It went more or less…his crew, the next operation, the next leave, the thirtieth mission, a training job. It would have been hurtful, especially for Marjorie, to mention this shortened perspective.

"Anyway," he added, "we've got to give them back some of their own medicine. For Coventry. For Johnno. For Kowalkowsky. For Archie Mitchell."

These were all men he'd trained and drunk beer with. They'd taken off alongside him but not come back. Their lockers had been quietly emptied to remove all trace of them except for what remained in other airmen's memories.

"But don't you get scared, Robert? Aren't you frightened of landing amongst them, the Germans, on your own and hurt. Don't you think about what they'd do to you?"

His father shuffled in his chair, irritated. This was his wife's worst nightmare, greater even than Robert being blown to bits in mid-air. Her dread was of him falling injured and in pain amongst those awful Germans. They would hate her only son. They would not help him. They would do unspeakable things to him.

Robert was sometimes frightened but he never admitted it. They were all frightened, terrified at times. There was plenty to be frightened of. Collision. Mechanical failure. Night fighters. Flak.

But there was a fear that kept all the others in check. The fear of being thought a coward. So when patriotism, a sense that this war was right, the desire for revenge… when all these failed, fear of being thought a coward got him through. He did not tell any of this to his parents.

"It's what I signed up for, Mother. Anyway, better to live one day as a lion than a lifetime as a lamb…"

She looked bemused. Lions? Lambs? What had that to do with anything? She was still worried. But she shut up. She went to get the tea-pot. She'd heard the latch on the gate lift.

« »

'Gentleman,' the Squadron Leader announced to the aircrews of 101 Squadron sitting, smoking, in the rows of hard chairs in the briefing room at Ludford Magna in Lincolnshire. '...ops are on for tonight and the target is... Mannheim.'

Mannheim elicited the standard groans. They'd have groaned if a weekend in Brighton had been announced. But they'd have settled for Mannheim as they entered the briefing room minutes earlier. It was well-defended but not the most-feared destination.

Not knowing the target was the worst position of all for the air crews. Now they knew, they could focus their minds. At least it wasn't Berlin, the one they all feared because it was so far away and so well-defended.

The briefing officer gave details of routes, bomb-loads, approaches, air defences, weather.

For Robert, Mannheim would be the 13th mission. This was considered a watershed number by the crews. It was enough air-time to know well what the dangers were. He had been through most of the gut-churning experiences at least once. The most common terror was the bombing approach, flying low through flak and smoke, laden with enough explosive to blast them to hell but not back, their plane illuminated by the burning city below and by search-lights. He'd always got through so far to the relief of a completed bombing run but his luck might not last forever.

Twelve missions was a respectable total for someone twenty years old. His reputation was growing and his own crew was feeling more confident in the lanky young man from the Yorkshire pits. He did not share with his crew that his secret was a tiny but very lucky piece of coal that he had brought with him from the mine. This went with him on all his missions, snug at the end of the index finger of his left flying glove, where he could press down and feel it at the start of every bombing run.

Twelve missions and a lucky piece of coal were not enough to make him complacent. The numbers did not encourage complacency. They all knew the maths even if they didn't think about it much. The prospects for these young men were truly awful.

Thirty missions was the magic number needed for a rest from operations. That was still an age away. Not an age away in time as measured by a clock or a calendar by the rest of us. That would pass quickly enough. Thirty missions was an age in air-crew time…the time spent waiting and worrying or in distractions between the surges of terror. This was why these men had such old, knowing eyes in their boyish faces.

The gloomy maths was also why Robert made copious notes during the remainder of the briefing, determined to try everything within his power to improve the dreadful odds that hung over them all like a curse. His crew liked him for this seriousness.

« »

As he waited for muster for the Mannheim mission, Robert wrote his regular letter to Marjorie in which he'd talk about everything but the anxiety gnawing in his gut.

Dear Marjorie,

I hope this letter finds you well. I am writing it whilst waiting for muster. I can't tell you more or I'd have the censor on my back. I suspect you'd rather not know. Anyway, I'll have rung and left a message with Aunt Maisie for you so that by the time you get this, you will already know that I am safe as, God Willing, I shall be.

I really enjoyed our weekend in Lincoln. I think you did, too. It was nice to have time to ourselves. And to live like toffs, if only for a weekend. It's always good to see you on home leave but with everyone fussing around, it's hard to get any time to ourselves. You deserved a nice trip away for all the worrying you do. I guess it's not easy being an airman's girl. We're a funny lot, I know, wrapped up in our own world, talking all the time about mates and stuff you don't know about.

Have you forgiven me yet for tricking you into the jewellers on false pretences? It was all better planned than a sortie to Berlin. Did you honestly think I would ever buy Dad cufflinks for his birthday? He'd chuck them back at me. "Not for the likes of me! Waste of b★★★★y money! What's wrong with buttons?"

You were so serious about choosing Dad the right pair. Just like you! But your face when the salesman brought out the tray of engagement rings, what a picture! I thought your eyes were going to pop. Do you know how much you blushed? It was well worth it, even the half crown I slipped the salesman to play along with it.

I hope you still like the ring. Too late now if you don't. You're stuck with it, and with me.

What about York next time? Can you get another Friday off before Christmas? I get a few days at home later this month if it's not cancelled at the last minute. Perhaps we can quietly plan a York trip then. We have an Engineer from York on the station. I'll ask him if he knows somewhere nice to stay. It would be hard to beat the White Hart in Lincoln but he'll know somewhere good and not too posh for your taste. You really need to get used to all that bowing and scraping for when you're married to a pilot after we've done with this lot in Germany.

So, signing off now. Got to get ready for you-know-what to you-don't-know-where. See you later in the month.

Yours Ever,
Robert

Having finished the letter, he tried to sleep a little until muster but found himself going over in his head key elements of the earlier briefing.

« »

An hour before dusk, Robert's crew gathered around him by their Lancaster one by one until it was complete. Conversation was minimal as men turned in on themselves and on their private rituals.

Minner disliked silence: "That dinner was bloody lovely tonight. Do you think they are trying to fatten us up for Christmas?"

"It's tomorrow's breakfast you should be thinking

about...Make sure you keep your eyes peeled for Fritz so we're all here to eat the bloody breakfast,' replied Ken, the navigator. 'Now shut up and get in your rabbit-hutch. And don't speak again unless you're telling us you've dropped a Messerschmitt."

The take-off was unremarkable for all but Minner at the tail of the plane. Most of the others had jobs to do on take-off. Minner always left his preparations until as late as possible to have something to distract him as the tension built. This left him time to gaze around from the glass turret as the Lancaster hurtled down the runway and heaved itself into the Lincolnshire sky. He should not have been so curious. He should have been preparing his guns for the battle to come.

Minner's gaze rested on a big black crow, sitting on one of the few remaining branches, jutting at right-angles from a dead tree. Its shoulders sloped desolately and its head was sunk down into its body. The crow was silhouetted against the darkening autumn sky, indifferent as the massive plane started its journey towards Europe and whatever awaited it. It spooked Minner but he didn't know why. He looked quickly away. He shuddered slightly from the chilly night.

Minner dare not tell the others what he'd seen. He fretted down to Beachy Head, over Northern France and on to Metz. It wore him out. He finally gave himself up to it as they crossed the border towards Mannheim. He accepted his fate, whatever it was. What else could he do? He had to get on with it now.

« »

Visibility was poor as they neared their target. When Robert was told by his navigator that they were over Mannheim, albeit a bit late, he dropped below the cloud for a sighting. There was no other RAF plane to be seen. His colleagues on the mission had been and gone. Robert's Lancaster must have drifted off course. Thankfully there were no German night-fighters. Theirs was the only plane in the sky. That made it the only target.

"Any idea where the bloody hell we are, Nav?" he asked over the intercom. Robert rarely swore or even raised his voice.

His navigator mumbled some excuse and pleaded for a bit of time to work out their exact location.

Minner knew where they were. From his gun-turret at the tail, he could see behind him a large area of flame and smoke created by the earlier bombing: "The target's about five miles behind us, to the south west. We should head for home, Skip. We're on our own. In a couple of minutes, we'll be lit up like the ballroom at the Ritz. Every Kraut this side of Berlin will be taking shots at us…"

There were murmurs of assent from others.

"That position seems to be correct, Skip. Do you want a course for home?" Ken asked.

There was no immediate reply. It would be hard to justify getting over the target and not delivering the bomb-load. He could go in from their present position. This might have some element of surprise. They could be in and out quickly. The night fighters would anyway be harrying the departing bombers back towards home.

Robert broke the silence. "We are going in. No course, Nav. I'll aim for the centre of the flames. Bombing positions everybody."

What the crew thought, they kept to themselves.

« »

Robert drew the Lancaster round and headed towards the flames. More and more light locked onto them as their plane trundled in to drop its payload. They were quickly coned at the centre of numerous beams of searchlight from all around Mannheim. It was roller-coaster time. The plane was buffeted by flak, hurled in fury towards the lumbering plane by every gun in Mannheim's defences but there was no choice but to see it through.

At last, the Bomb-Aimer uttered the longed-for words: "Bombs away, Skip! Bombs away!"

Robert forced the nose up immediately to gain some protection from the cloud cover.

« »

The worst might be over, but there were plenty of dangers ahead. First, they had to escape the air defences around Mannheim, then cross the border into occupied France and turned northwards. They skirted Metz. With each mile, the tension eased slightly. They could at least hope for the best now.

Just north of Metz, the mid-upper gunner spotted tracer fire from what turned out to be a Messerschmitt 109 returning from its pursuit of the departed bombers. The gunner returned fire as the fighter bore down on them. There was no hit and the fighter disappeared from the gunner's line of sight.

"Corkscrew port! Corkscrew port now!" screamed the gunner.

Robert turned the Lancaster's nose into this well-rehearsed manoeuvre, diving and twisting to port and then banking steeply to do it all again, hoping desperately that they had shaken off their pursuer. Every minute they flew on without the fighter re-appearing increased their hopes that they had given him the slip. After twenty minutes, long aircrew minutes, they thought they had a clear run for home.

Rear-gunner Minner, with the memory of the black crow re-forming in his mind, was the first to know different.

Toul, France.

After waiting so long to visit, their arrival at the cemetery had come upon the man's sister, Dorothy, and Marjorie, his ex-fiancé, in a rush. They felt flustered.

The cemetery was a neat square, cut from the surrounding fields. The sight of row after row of white headstones hushed them instantly. The headstones stood ram-rod straight in ordered lines, forming a square around a central memorial like those in every town and village in England. The grass was neatly cut and the flower-beds well-tended. It was a sunny, early-Autumn morning. The road skirting the cemetery was silent now that the old Citroen taxi had chugged its way to the brow of the hill and dropped out of sight, back towards the town. The only sound was birdsong rising to the clear blue sky from the hedges around the cemetery. It was a respectful and peaceful sight.

The two women walked tentatively through the iron-gate, Marjorie linking her friend's arm. A few paces inside the gate, Dorothy passed the bunch of red and white roses to her friend to hold whilst she took out the letter from the War Graves Commission with the grave number and cemetery plan on it. After rotating the plan several times, she got her bearings and they both set off, still in silence, towards four rows of headstones to the left of the entrance.

No matter how much time had passed since his parents received the telegram, nor how often they had thought of this moment, when they finally stumbled on his grave and read his name, both women gasped and came to an immediate halt. They stood before the headstone, arm-in-arm and in silence, both of them shocked anew after all these years. Tears welled in their eyes. Marjorie began to cry openly. A sob grew in Dorothy's chest. She tried to stifle it but, finally, the sob escaped in a low moan.

Now it was real. It had all happened. There was no other explanation for his long absence from their lives.

Their airman had been blasted out of the sky over France. His beautiful young body had been unceremoniously dragged by one ankle, limp and broken from the wreckage of his plane by enemies who hated him, thought him a 'terror pilot'. He had then lain in a cold grave, far from home and unvisited for years, never knowing if the war he believed in so strongly had been won or lost.

They read and re-read the inscription to finally exclude all doubt:

Robert James Sutcliffe
Killed in Action over Metz, France
23rd September 1943
Flying Officer (Pilot) Aged 20
'Greater Love Hath no Man than This,
That he Lay Down his Life for his Friends'

In time their composure returned. They began to deliver their messages to him, their thoughts of him from the intervening years. They told him that he had been loved very much. They hoped he had known that. They told him he was still loved, especially by his family, and would never be forgotten. They told him how sorry they were not to have visited his grave before now and hoped he understood why. They told him he was honoured in his village and still talked about with respect and affection. That he was the only pilot on the village war memorial. This was all true.

They also told him the war had been won and that

the world was grateful that Hitler had been defeated. That Hitler had been even more of a monster than they'd known at the point when Robert had been killed, what with the discovery of the death-camps and so on. This was also true.

In their hearts they were not sure we were making a good fist of the peace that he had helped to create. They could not bring themselves to re-assure him that he had not died in vain. His own belief in the war had never wavered, but their sense of loss had been so great that they could not see beyond their grief to the greater good of the defeat of Nazism.

But all this history was not why they were there. They were there to remember and to remind. To remember Robert and to remind others, anyone passing, maybe only the French gardener, to whom all the graves were pretty much the same, that this was a man whose family had not forgotten him.

Dorothy knelt down and half-buried the vase they'd brought with them all the way from Yorkshire in the fine, French soil. Marjorie fetched some water from a tap nearby. They put the roses, red for the love they both felt for him and white for his Yorkshire roots, into the vase one by one, each woman in turn until they were all in place. They then stood back a little, bowed their heads and muttered their final words to their dead airman. They turned in unison for the gate and for the walk down the quiet road back to Toul.

Now they'd done what they set out to do, they felt

flat and weary. It had been a long journey for them and so different from the one that had brought Robert himself to this piece of French countryside. They thought about the ordeal he'd endured on that fateful night as they themselves strolled down this quiet country road with only the birdsong from the blue sky above as background to their thoughts.

Some Kind of Love Story

"It's a boy, May. A big bouncing boy. Do you want him now or shall I clean him up a bit?"

May rolls over gingerly to put her face to the bedroom wall: "I don't want it."

Nurse Moore thinks to herself 'Well, May, dear. You should have thought about what you wanted and didn't want nine months ago. It's not sale or return.' But the midwife doesn't say any of this.

"Right. I'll clean him up a bit first, shall I?" It's not a question really. She begins to bathe the baby in an enamel bowl while the Doctor prepares the sutures.

Nurse Moore finishes washing and drying the baby, wraps him up and then takes him downstairs, out of the way whilst the Doctor does his bit. She knows she makes him nervous and it's better for all concerned if he can fumble away unobserved by her knowing eye.

"Do you want to hold him, Joan? It is Joan, isn't it?" the midwife asks as she strides into the front room with the new-born.

Does she want to hold him? She can't wait.

"Yes please," Joan says, trying to suppress a wide grin, trying to look grown-up enough to hold her baby brother.

"Be careful. He's quite an armful. Your mother never has it easy, does she?"

Joan doesn't answer. She doesn't understand the question.

The midwife puts the baby carefully into the girl's arms, which sag under the weight. She has to shuffle him a bit higher. One of the baby's podgy arms is thrusting out from his wrappings. Joan stares in wonderment at the round, blotchy face of her third brother.

"Keep him warm, dear. Near the fire. But don't try to stand up with him. Shout me if you need anything. I'm just going back to help the doctor finish off."

She turns and sets off back up the stairs in her starched blue uniform, trimmed with white. She'd put the white cap on the sideboard when she'd originally burst in an hour or so ago, ready for the fray. It lies there still. Joan had wondered about quickly trying it on while the midwife was busy with her mum but the chance is gone now.

Help the doctor finish off, the midwife had said. Do it herself, more like. Fat lot of good he's been so far. Turning up late. Big gangling youth, he is. He looks as though he's been sent on ahead to tell them that the doctor, the real one, will be along shortly. But this is the real one. Just qualified. First job, first baby and it's one of May's specials.

He knows which is the business-end but probably not much more. He's had no need to take his jacket off though. The cuffs of his sports-coat are half way up his fore-arms, well away from the messy stuff. Still, at least he doesn't pretend he knows it all. Very deferential to Nurse

Moore, he is. Quite right too, even though she says it herself. She'll lick him into shape soon enough, like the others before him.

The baby had finally popped out, all twelve pounds of him, just after midnight. On reflection, she's not sure "popped out" is the phrase May would use. The doctor's eyes had stood out like chapel hat-pegs. All he could say was:

"They weren't this big in the medical books!"

May's face was a picture at that.

Good job May and the midwife know what they're doing. May's fourth... fifth if you count the still-birth. And the midwife's? Well. How many is it? She's no idea. Five of May's and hundreds, nay thousands more besides. They are all hers in these pit villages.

May's are always big babies. It really doesn't get any easier for her, especially not now she's nearly forty. She's a bit of a mess. She needs stitches again.

"We should have fitted you with a zip after the first, May," the midwife says after the worst is over. "It would have saved us all a lot of trouble."

May smiles a weak smile.

Months earlier, she'd confided to the midwife that she was disappointed she'd caught on again. Nurse Moore had heard this many times. It's a worry for May and her husband, coming later in their lives, a good few years after the last. It's another mouth to feed and another body to clothe. That's even harder, what with rationing and all.

It's a big deal because they were just getting turned round after the war. All three older kids are at school now. The pits are newly nationalised…"Managed by the NCB *for* the people." It's not just a slogan. They believe it. And now they all have the new National Health Service. Things are looking up.

Then this baby. It's a bit of a set-back.

Like most, she and Alf probably don't have a plan. Who does? They simply work hard and hope for the best. Things just happen to folk like them. Things like the war just ended. And still-births. And nice stuff sometimes. But if they'd had a plan, this baby would not have been in it.

Nurse Moore hasn't spoken to May about these feelings since that first chat. What have feelings got to do with anything? What can't be cured must be endured. That's what got them through the war. It will get them through the peace. Anyway, Nurse Moore just senses that May has softened gradually during the pregnancy and has finally managed to convince herself that she secretly wanted another girl all the time. She'd definitely had enough of boys, though. About a month earlier, she'd chosen a girl's name, Jennifer, after Jennifer Jones the film star, but she has no boy's name ready.

Down in the warm front room, Joan may look as though she thinks her new brother has just landed from Mars but she knows different. She's twelve after all. She knows and hears much more than the adults think.

In April of that year, her mother had sat the three of them down, her and her two younger brothers, to tell them of the coming baby. The three children had dutifully sat in ascending age on the sofa that Joan was sitting on now.

"I've got something to tell you," their mother started when she had their full attention. "We're going to have another baby!"

The boys were silent, not really knowing what it meant for them. They just squirmed and grinned at each other.

Joan was more composed. She took the wind right out of her mother's sails. It took just two words:

"I know."

"You know! How do you know?"

"I heard you and dad argu…talking about it."

"What did you hear?" Her mother was feigning a lack of concern but had coloured slightly.

"You were talking about whose fault it was. Can it be someone's fault? Having a baby I mean?"

May ignored the question.

"What else did you hear then? You know what happens to little pigs with big ears, young madam?"

"I can't remember anything else," Joan lied. "It was ages ago. I thought you must have been wrong. I'd forgotten about it."

She hadn't forgotten about it. She'd thought about it every day and was dying to tell her best friend Pauline but knew it was more than her life was worth. Now it was out.

Her mother left it there. She knew it could have been worse. She'd probe a bit more when she and Joan were on their own.

There's a noise at the kitchen door and in comes Alf, cradling a sleepy boy in the crook of both arms. They are followed by Grandma Lawson. May's mother is lean but upright still despite her eighty years. They've all been together at her house in the next street, out of the way. Alf and the two boys almost fill the doorway but Grandma pushes past them straight into the front room:

"Let me have him, Joan love. Let me give you a rest."

Joan's happy to hand him over. She's not dared move for fear of breaking the baby somehow and her arms are aching. Her Grandma takes him on her knee and squeezes and feels him all over…his limbs, his spine…checking him out. She stares at his face and deep into his eyes, smitten. Spoiling her grandchildren is her indulgence after all the hard years with her own eight, when there'd been no time for spoiling.

"Well, that's a bit of a turn-up," she says. "A boy after all! Don't know why your mother was so sure it was a girl. You get what you're given. At least he looks healthy." She turns to the new-born: " Yes my love. You do, don't you!"

"Have you got a boy's name, Alf?" Grandma Lawson asks. "Caught you on the hop, this little chap."

The new dad says nothing. He looks down at his third son. He brushes the boy's cheek with a big finger. What he feels, no one knows. But he'll do all the things a dad has to do, quietly, with no fuss.

Grandma Lawson knows it won't be up to Alf to name the boy. That will be for May. He rather blotted his copybook when Martin was born. He came up with *Winston* as a middle name totally off his own bat on the way to register him. This was an act of patriotism coming as it did in the middle of the war. It is not the most helpful thing in this pit village for young Martin to be named after the man who sent the troops into Wales against the miners.

May will be more judicious. She'll want to avoid the names of any of these Australian cricketers that have just trounced England. It was all Alf could talk about for a while. She suspects one of these players' names would be in Alf's head for a boy. Keith Miller. Don Bradman. It will be none of these if May has anything to do with it. And she will.

Alf goes up the stairs to see his wife. He knocks nervously on the door and waits to be invited into his own bedroom.

"Come in. It's a shop!" Nurse Moore shouts, very much in charge as the young Doctor packs away his instruments.

It's a good job Alf hadn't been around earlier, Nurse Moore thinks. Good that he'd not heard what May said when they'd told her it was a boy. But she isn't worried for this baby. May is made of the right stuff. A strong woman with clear views and a sharp way of putting things.

A good mother. The other three children are healthy and bright and well-behaved. Food on the table is a priority over anything else. May is ambitious that her kids make something of themselves. Most of all, they shouldn't go anywhere near the pit. They're all doing well at school. Some in the village think she has ideas above her station but she doesn't care what they think. She does feel a bit above it all.

Nurse Moore knows it's finally time. She goes and retrieves the baby and brings him briskly up the stairs. She plops him into May's arms.

May looks down at the round red face, its lips pursing as if with indigestion. May's face slowly warms into a smile: "Oh. He's beautiful. Beautiful!"

That wouldn't have been Nurse Moore's description, even after she's cleaned him up. But it's a good sign. Love's blind. It's obviously love.

Treats

I'd always tried my best to be a good little boy. I couldn't vouch for my nappy stage. I couldn't remember that. It was yonks ago. But I was old enough now to know that two weeks before Christmas was not the moment to stop being good.

I'd seen enough Christmases by now to know all the stuff we did to get ready for it. I started reminding mum about it all the time:

"When are we going to …?"

"Shouldn't we be …?"

"The Briggs have already…!"

I liked it all. Pickling the onions and red cabbage with my father. I even liked the vinegary smell tickling my nostrils. I liked cranking the handle on the mincing machine that churned out the sweet mixture that would fill the mince-pies. I could manage with just one hand this year. As a reward for every bowl filled, my mother let me poke my finger into the sweet mince-meat and get a bit to taste.

I loved it when Mum got the step-ladder out and started stringing the paper trimmings across the ceiling. My chest swelled when I had to pass her something. I was helping. I was useful. Best of all, I remembered where every bauble was meant to go on the mantelpiece, to the inch. Even my mother sometimes forgot that but I could put her right.

Near to Christmas Day, I hated watching my mother pulling the insides out of the bird we'd got for our Christmas dinner. I hated it but I still watched every bit of slop dragged out.

This year Mum had promised me that I alone could help her decorate the tree. We would do it when the others were at school.

First, she took out the tree from the back of the wardrobe. It was a battered old thing. It was much older than me. It was a bit taller, too. It had tin feet and a spiky tip. My mother folded out the wire branches one by one. She turned the whole tree round so that the barest branches were out of sight at the back.

The tree took pride of place on the dining table by the window in the best room. It was better than the plastic roses that usually stood there. I asked my mother why we couldn't have the tree there all year but she just laughed.

Anyway, the tree was never moved until twelfth night or something. It didn't matter. We never ate at the dining table anyway. It was just for show, Mum said. Just to look posh. Even at Christmas, we ate in the kitchen.

I knew all the Christmas-tree decorations. My mother sometimes bought one or two new ones but most of the decorations were my old friends. I recognised them as soon as she took them out of the cardboard box that they had lived in all year and unwrapped them from the newspaper. She laid them all out and then asked me for them by name. I was really quick. The names were our secret. Only we knew them all. We didn't tell the others.

There was *Polly,* the bird-of-paradise. Her tail-feathers were a bit grubby but the rest of her was still glittery. She reminded me of those Tiller Girl dancers on TV on Saturday nights. She clipped to a branch and rocked on a spring. There was *Santa* on a sleigh drawn by Rudolf. We had lots of candle-holders. I helped Mum clip these onto the branches. Mum made me move some to the front to fill it out.

"Nobody will see them at the back," she said.

My mother topped the tree with *Dainty*, the fairy, in her frilly dress. I didn't like touching *Dainty* for fear of breaking her. Anyway, she was a bit girly.

Finally, I passed my mother the chocolate figures and coins, wrapped in foil, to hang on the tree one by one. These chocolate figures were new each year because we kids always ate them on Christmas Eve, once we were all ready for bed.

When the last one had been hung, Mum told me that under no circumstances should I eat any of the figures until Christmas Eve:

"There are twelve figures, three for each of you. As the littlest, you will pick your favourite three first. Then the others can have their turn. OK?"

She'd spelled out what would happen if I snaffled one. My presents would be sent to those poor children in Africa. And I'd spend Christmas Day in the bedroom. No chicken dinner.

I was angry that she was telling me this. She should tell the others. I was a good boy. I needed no second telling, but I got one anyway.

I knew she meant it. She put a mouse trap on top of the pickle-jar last year when onions kept going missing. It wasn't me. I couldn't reach them. I made sure she knew that. She told my brothers what she'd done but one of them still ended up bawling with a mouse-trap on his finger.

"Under no circumstances. Do you understand?"

"No Mum. I won't. I promise."

« »

I stared at the chocolate figures dangling just above my nose every day. I flicked them with my finger to send them spinning on their strings. I could taste the chocolate. Christmas chocolate wasn't like the stuff we ate the rest of the year. It was so good. I could eat it until I was sick. I had done last year.

I knew where all twelve figures were on the tree and could have found them to order, blindfolded. I would picture them at night in bed. I had made a selection in my mind early and stuck to it through the build-up to Christmas Eve. It wasn't just about picking the biggest shapes. Some I just liked. I also had to make sure my picks were within my reach. I didn't want my brothers or sister touching them first even if they were being helpful by reaching them for me. I wanted to get them off the tree myself.

I'd chosen the reindeer, the fat bird and the king. I'd even worked out the best order to eat them in. My mouth filled with spit at the thought.

« »

We were all bathed and in our new pyjamas on Christmas Eve. Dad was just back from the Miners Welfare Club. He was in a good mood. I dragged him in and sat him down because he was dawdling in the kitchen and we were all waiting to scoff our chocolate.

"Fire the start gun!" Dad said as he flopped down in the arm-chair.

My mother *finally* consented to the chocolate feast beginning.

My brothers and sister sat in a line on the sofa at the opposite end of the room from the tree. They watched me go first. I rushed to the tree, almost tripping over my overlong pyjama trousers. I pulled off the reindeer and peeled back the foil. My eyes popped wide; my mouth dropped open. It was empty.

Mum looked on: "It might just be a dud. Try the next one love."

I threw down the screwed up foil, detached the king figure and peeled back the foil. Another dud. My eyes brimmed with tears. I turned away so they couldn't see.

I snatched the fat bird from its branch. I almost dragged the Christmas tree over with it. I quickly peeled back the foil.

Empty!

I threw down the crumpled foil.

I turned to my brothers and sister. My sister was blushing; one brother was staring down at his slippers, the other was grinning like a monkey. There was a tiny flake of chocolate in the corner of his mouth. I felt my teeth grinding. I clenched both fists. I turned to the tree and swept it off the table with my arm.

I burst into tears.

Rite of Passage

By the time they'd reached the pit-yard, half the village was there. Women with toddlers and babes in arms, older children of Paul's age as well as youths all lined the top end of the yard, two and three deep for most of its length. It was one of the biggest days in the village year…the Friday in August when the mine closed down for the summer holiday. Men and ponies both had the prospect of two weeks rest, the ponies in a nearby field, the men and their families at the seaside. The crowd had a good view towards the exit from which the ponies would emerge. It was always a good show.

The ponies had been underground for a whole year. They'd smelled no fresh air, nor seen any natural light in that time. They'd certainly not seen so many people at one go. It was another hot sunny day and so the bright light would flood their eyes and spook them.

There were so many ponies to lead to the field a mile away that it was a case of all hands on deck. Boys were allowed to lead the quieter, smaller ponies. Men and older youths would lead or try to ride the wilder ones bareback with only a bridle to cling to.

Paul and his mates had made a pact that year that they would lead a pony to the field. They were old enough now, soon to be secondary school pupils, so it was time to prove themselves. They discussed what sort of pony they wanted.

In his heart of hearts Paul didn't really want to take one at all. Animals weren't his strong point. But he simply couldn't afford to back down. His mates were starting to think he was a bit of a swot. Not quite one of them. He was getting ideas above his station. He racked his brains for the name of a nice gentle old pony from last year.

"Has Luke come up yet?" he asked the tall youth next to him, once he'd slipped his way through to the front of the crowd.

The youth was drawing deep on his Park Drive. He was not going to be hurried by this bit of a kid. He blew out a cloud of blue-grey smoke, more it seemed than he could possibly have inhaled.

"Came up this morning with the other sheep." He didn't give Paul so much as a look. He spat a small piece of tobacco from his bottom lip.

"Sheep?" Paul asked.

"Aye. Sheep. Tame things for kids like thee to lead" He still hadn't deigned to look at Paul. "It's t'nasty bastards they bring up this afternoon. That's what I'm here for."

It had just got worse for Paul. He'd missed the sheep. He'd have to take a nasty bastard. He wished it were tomorrow and he were miles away, on holiday at the coast. Anywhere but waiting here to be trampled into the road by a rampaging pony. He stared ahead, eyes glazed.

« »

The wheels on the pit head gear span slowly, quickened in mid-lift, and then slowed again as the cage neared the top of the shaft. The crowd hushed and turned from their conversations to see what beast would emerge from the bowels of the earth next.

The ponies came up in pairs but tethered and separated in the divided cage to limit any damage they could do to one another or themselves once they were catapulting, blind as bats, through the stale air of the pit shaft. This journey was not made often enough for them to ever get used to it.

One of the horse keepers always led the pair of ponies out of the cage and into the light. It needed a good horseman to hold and calm the animals as they met fresh air, daylight, open-space and the noise of the gathered crowd in one rush. They reared and pulled, their eyes bulging, their nostrils flared. Their legs splayed and their feet slid and sparked as they clattered on the concrete floor and the metal tub-tracks.

On this lift it was Tommy and Buster. Tommy was O.K. but Buster was a nasty bastard. The crowd went quiet. They knew Buster of old. He hurt someone just about every year.

The horse keeper settled the two a bit but Buster kept pulling his head back to eye the crowd.

Many pony drivers loved and cared for their ponies but it was a hard environment that these animals operated in. There was danger for both men and beasts. There was coal to get out and a bonus to be won, and if ponies had off-days and jeopardised the men's earnings, then they might know about it. There was little room for sentiment. Few ponies avoided a bit of mistreatment at some stage. Some were cowed by this and learned to get by.

Buster was different. The more he was chastised, the more difficult he became, prompting more ill-treatment in a cycle that left him defiant and deranged, constantly on the look-out for chances to kick or bite.

He had on a rough, leather skull-cap worn for protection down the pit. His name was chalked across the front. Where his eyes should have been, there were just two round, dark holes cut in the skull-cap. He could watch you, but you couldn't see his eyes.

No one had stepped forward to lead either of these ponies. The keeper was getting impatient. It was hard work hanging onto them. The crowd started to buzz and necks craned to look up and down the ranks to see who dared to step forward.

"They're all scared of thi, Buster." one woman shouted. "They're only brave when they've had a skin full of ale!"

A few of her friends nodded agreement.

Buster reared away from the keeper.

The tall youth beside Paul stepped out of the crowd. All eyes turned on him. He didn't stop to take in the admiring looks. He'd seen enough cowboy films to know you fixed your fate in the eye and walked straight towards it. He was still smoking his Park Drive. He took the butt from his mouth and examined it closely to confirm that there was nothing he could smoke further. Without breaking his stride, he crushed the remnant of his cig between thumb and index finger and cast it aside in a shower of sparks. His eyes were fixed on Buster.

Buster was going through his repertoire. At the moment, he was prancing more or less on the same spot. The keeper's patience had been sorely tried and his arms were tiring from hanging onto Buster and the less fractious Tommy. He was relieved to see this youth coming towards him, Buster in his sights.

The youth was out to make a name by fettling Buster. Tommy was really quite a "sheep", everyone knew that. A right little lamb, if the truth be known. If the youth were right, and it was the nasty bastards brought up in the afternoon, then Tommy was as good as it would get.

Paul took his chance. Out he strode, falling in about ten yards behind the lanky youth, nervous but feeling he'd worked a flanker on his mates who'd have to take a really mean beast or lose face.

Buster stopped his prancing. He faced the approaching youth head on. He was adept at getting in a kick or a bite in the most confined of places down the pit so manoeuvring in the pit-yard was easy for him. As the youth neared him, Buster moved sideways on and aimed a speculative kick with his hind legs that was strong enough to break a man's thigh.

It did not connect. But it was near enough for the youth. His courage was blown away by the draught from that kick. He skirted Buster, and before the keeper could react, he'd grabbed Tommy's lead-rope and was off down the pit-yard, followed by hoots of derision from the crowd.

"Stop and milk it, why don't you, you nesh git!"

Paul stopped in his tracks. His mouth gaped open. It felt as if the kick aimed at the youth had removed his stomach. What was it to be…trampled to a messy death by Buster, his innards spread across the pit-yard, or a lifetime's humiliation from his mates?

"Well, are you going to stand there like a wimp?" asked the keeper. "Are you man enough or not?"

The keeper knew Paul. He was a decent sort.

"Look," he muttered for Paul alone to hear. "Hold on tight and stay close as long as you can, but if he gets any room to move, let the sod go. He'll find his own way to the field."

"Come on, Paul!" someone shouted from the crowd. "Hi, ho Silver!"

"Even money he breaks thi' neck, young Paul!"

"Leave us thi' bike in thi' Will, Paul" one of his mates shouted.

If he turned round now, he faced a lifetime of this. Paul took a deep breath and grabbed the rope as tight by Buster's skull-cap as he could. He hung on with all his weight, as near as he could get to Buster's front legs without being trampled.

The crowd cheered as they made their way out of the pit-yard and out of sight, Buster trotting twenty to the dozen and Paul hanging on and digging his heels in to slow things down as much as he could. His mates looked on in disbelief and a little envy.

Maybe Buster took pity on him. Maybe he just wanted to get some of that sweet, juicy grass between his yellow teeth. In any case, he spared Paul the worst.

Paul managed to hang on around the stocky pony's neck until they were well out of sight of the crowd in the pit-yard. His strength was draining with every yard travelled until he felt he could hold on no more. At one final shake of Buster's neck, Paul let the rope slip through his burning palms. It was a weakening of will as much as strength. Anyhow, he'd done enough.

Buster didn't hang around. He was off as fast as his legs would carry him to his two weeks of being an ordinary pony, doing what ponies do.

Paul rubbed his hands to ease the stinging from the rope burn. He looked around. No-one could have seen what had happened. Anyway, stronger men than he had baulked at the challenge. He'd got half way to the field. He wouldn't go back and tell them he'd not made it. Let them find out if they could. They'd all have forgotten about today by the time he got back from the seaside.

He'd be too old for donkey-rides this year.

Half Empty

April had been miserable in just about every way. News programmes and weather forecasts had competed with one another to broadcast the bleakest possible outlook for Britain. Robert Peston came on TV daily to taunt the nation in his know-all sort of way with the worst budget deficit since the Great Depression.

All the time Peston was live on air, strutting his gloomy stuff, Helen Willetts stood in the newsroom wings, smirking and thinking to herself: 'Not terrible enough Robert. You'll have to do better (or is it worse?) than that.' She'd finally step forward in front of her weather charts and trump Peston's piece with record rainfall figures and depressions, deeper even than the 1930s. Deeper than ever.

It was difficult for people to know what was more disheartening, the gathering gloom over the European economy or the constant cold rain, slanting down countrywide? The answer depended on whether people had to go to the bank in the hope the bank would still be there or whether they needed to brave the downpour to take a fretting dog for a long-delayed walk. Otherwise, the bulletins throughout April were equally depressing. What on earth could Britons have done to deserve this awful fate? Who had killed that bloody robin?

« »

May finally lifted half of the gloom by delivering some wonderful summer weather. Temperatures soared to the late twenties. The summer-blue skies were scoured only by occasional jet vapour. The jets that were tracing vapour across the sky were full of Brits whose nerve had finally been broken by the gloom in April. They'd booked panic flights to get them away from the impending catastrophe to just about anywhere that wasn't here. Their problem now was that many of the destinations chosen were actually colder and more bankrupt than the Britain they were escaping from.

For those with stiffer upper lips who stayed at home, the heat had built up over seven successive days of Mediterranean temperatures. Today was hot, too, but a covering of cloud had crept in overnight and was acting like the lid of a clay oven, pressing the heat down and allowing no relieving breeze. It was oppressive and sapping.

William sat in his garden and baked. He was grumpy. He *should* have been enjoying the weather. But he felt oddly ill at ease. Not himself. He was hot, listless and irritable. He had a free day. Another one. He could do anything he wanted.

But the things that suggested themselves or were suggested by his wife, Helen, before she left the house that morning, he simply did not want to do. In truth, he thought she left with an over-the-top show of enthusiasm. Quite disturbing so early in the morning. So now he sat and sweltered and felt grumpy with himself for frittering away such a lovely day. Such a gift of a day. It was a day he would have died for in the middle of April.

The radio was on in the kitchen. The volume was finely set, purposely just audible to him in the garden through an open door. He didn't want to listen to what was on at that moment. Absolute drivel, hence the low volume. But he might want to hear what came on later, hence just enough volume for him to pick out a phrase or topic or a familiar voice that might ignite his interest. Helen invariably banged on that the sensible thing to do would have been to look at the radio programme for the day and make some choices: "*Positive* choices!"

She always stressed the word positive, as though it was the most important word in the language. It was her favourite word. He was sick of it. It signified one end of a battery terminal to him but she spat it out of her narrow lips like it was a poisoned dart. Anyway, she was out shopping. Making choices. Positive ones, no doubt.

Being organised like she was needed too much effort for his taste. It was a form of vanity, he was sure of that. As though her time was too important to squander. Absolute tosh. So he stuck with his tried and tested method of just letting things happen around him as they may.

He was fairly comfortable in his padded garden chair. It would take something momentous to move him today. A house fire. An invasion by aliens. The collapse of the Euro.

Well, probably not the latter. While he could just about imagine the first two, he still had absolutely no idea what the collapse of the Euro would look like. Would buildings fall down around them? Would hitherto civilised people beat one another's brains out for the last loaf in Waitrose? Would people be reduced to eating rats, nettle soup or Iceland pizzas? Would cash machines be programmed to laugh in your face when you tried to take money out?

William remained ignorant despite Robert Peston's tutorials on the issue that were beamed daily into the nation's living rooms, courtesy of the BBC. He was sure in Peston's notes, these tutorials were secretly subtitled "The Financial Crisis for Dummies like You. Yes. You!" He listened to them intently. He was *trying* to understand. Peston's tone was oddly relaxed, even as he unfolded the worst of the dreadful story. It was as if he'd already moved his money somewhere safe but he sure as hell wasn't going to let the rest of us in on it. Try as he might, William couldn't work out how the collapse would roll out, nor what it would mean for him. Except of course that it would not be nice. That much at least he'd gleaned from Peston's sadistic delivery of the ever-worsening news.

He decided to put up with the drone of the half-heard radio, even though it clashed slightly with the bird-song from the thick hedges that surrounded his garden. The hedges, by the way, badly need trimming. The sight of them was an intrusion into his peace of mind, another reminder of what he *should* be doing. But it was just one of the many tasks that he positively did not want to do.

It was a long list, the *should-do list* but it was simply not, in his mind, a *should-do day.* Such chores were not a fair reward for the misery endured through April. He decided to blank out the intrusion that the unkempt hedge represented.

He just needed to move the chair a few degrees to an angle that took the hedge outside his line of sight. There. Sorted. What a relief! This movement took a little effort. Effort that he should really have devoted to chilling out. But it was worth it, on balance.

The dog was panting beside him. Thankfully, he was too listless to want a walk. He was usually such a fearless slayer of anything small that came within his range. But not that day. He'd hardly noticed three or four insects buzzing round him. He'd declared a heat-induced amnesty. He stirred. He just about mustered enough energy to drag his frame to better shade where he could doze the day away until the cool of evening.

"That's my boy! We're getting old and lazy together."

William glanced to his left. It was a mistake. Under the apple tree, he spotted the strewn garden tools he'd used yesterday to tidy some flower beds. The job took him over an hour! It was a good move though. He was finishing just as Helen came back from the W.I. so it looked as though he'd been busy all day. It was always good to save a job to be doing just as she got home.

She'd been going to WI rather a lot recently. He didn't know they met so often but, anyway, he was left in peace and she invariably came back flushed and re-energised and generally stayed out of his way for a while, humming and smiling to herself.

He'd felt so virtuous at removing a task from the should-do list in yesterday's blistering sun that he'd excused himself from putting the tools back in the shed when he'd finished. Why do today what you can put off until tomorrow? That was his motto. Ramming them back into the shed was always a pain because it was invariably crammed full of junk. It badly needed a good sorting out. This sort-out was another activity from the *should-do list*. But it wasn't a job for that fateful day either. It would have to wait until he'd cut the bloody grass anyway, also a task to put off until another day.

No. He deserved better after all the worrying he'd done recently over Europe. Who else was going to worry for the nation if not him? People were all so busy holding onto their jobs. Leave it to him. He was good at it. It just wasn't the right sort of activity for a hot day in the garden. The best thing about worrying was that it could be done sitting down, with closed eyes or, with luck, even asleep.

He shifted his chair again slightly so that he now also excluded the abandoned tools from his line of sight, as well as the unkempt hedges. This needed precise geometry but he managed it.

His current book lay on the little garden table beside his chair looking a bit tempting. But it wasn't tempting enough. He'd started it that very morning, flush with energy. Well, 'flush' might have been an overstatement.

It was a famous book. One that everybody *should* read at some time in their life. But he just couldn't get going. It was already 3pm but he was only four pages into it. Poor progress for three hours in the garden. He was a forty page an hour man usually. But not on this of all days.

Such a bloody fuss about a married woman who fell in love with a dashing but feckless cavalry officer. Honestly! Nothing to get so worked up about. "Get over it!" he felt like saying to her scandalised husband and friends and indeed to her. He couldn't care less. Let them get on with it, do their worst, but leave him out of it. She should chuck herself under a train or something. Preferably by the end of chapter one so he didn't have to plough through the remaining wedge of pages. He was simply not interested. He had his own agenda, even if there was nothing on it.

He took a sip from the tumbler of water on the garden table beside his chair. It was half empty, of course. What else would it be? It was a half empty sort of day. Maybe he was a half empty sort of guy.

He really just wanted to doze and wake. Doze and wake. Wake and doze the day away. That was better. He lowered the back of his chair into the recline position. He needed that after the exertion of half an hour's worry about the Euro.

He was dragged back to semi-consciousness by a strange, flushing heat spreading up into his face from his neck. He needed a drink. He reached for his tumbler of water. A pain was spreading down his outstretched arm. His numb fingers knocked the half-full glass off the table onto the grass. He jerked upright and perched on the edge of his chair, waiting for the pain to subside but it didn't. He eventually slumped back into the chair, his head flopping to one side as he slipped away.

The empty glass lay at his feet, its contents now fully soaked into the uncut grass.

Second Chance

Straight out of university, James had completed a short course on how to teach English as a foreign language. He must have done well because he landed the plumb posting. Rome.

The teaching was interspersed with sipping espresso on the Piazza del Popolo, trying to look cool and mysterious whilst watching beautiful women parade by. His students at the Business College were young, mostly in their late teens or early twenties, often quite anglophile in outlook and, best of all for a young man of only twenty four, they were predominantly female. He was a walking English lesson so he was invited to whatever party or outing was taking place on evenings and weekends. It had seemed to him at the time much better than force-feeding Shakespeare to adolescents in some deadbeat comprehensive.

But it was soon to end. He would be leaving for England in January to take up a teaching post in Oxfordshire and finally to get on with what he called "real life". He thought he was ready. Although the Italians had recently discovered rugby, so he could play that occasionally here in Italy, his other love, tennis, was very exclusive in Rome and prohibitively expensive. English summer evenings in the bar after a good game pulled very strongly at his heart and he'd decided he could live without them no more.

His final social outing was to attend the New Year's Eve party for staff and students of the Business College in Rome where he'd taught. As he looked from the edge of the dance floor at the exuberance of the party, he was beginning to wonder why he'd declined the offer of a further year. But he had. He was leaving.

Most of his students had come to the party, knowing it was their last chance to say farewell to their young English teacher. He was trying to work out who was missing. He scanned the room slowly, smiling to himself. He would miss them. They were funny, lively, generous. Bruno. Luca. Bene. Allegra. Isabella. Even the painfully shy Elena had made an effort to come to an event that was not really her scene, just to say goodbye.

Then, just as midnight approached, in strode Francesca, majestic beyond her years. He'd not expected her to attend. He assumed she'd be at some swish affair elsewhere.

Heads turned to the newcomer. No wonder. The blond curls and oval face. The pout, glossed in dramatic red lipstick. The elegant figure that seemed her birthright. She was always so assured. All the male students were under her spell, the females wary and jealous. Even he, as class teacher, had been a bit in awe of her.

Head high, shoulders back, she came straight towards him, parting the crowd of revellers along the way. She stopped square in front of him.

"Hi James," she said, her head now tilted to one side. In her party heels, she was almost as tall as him. "Just wanted to say farewell. It's been really nice to know you."

"Thank you, Francesca. Thank you for coming. Thank you so much."

He shuffled nervously, not knowing what to do or say next. Francesca knew. She raised herself slightly onto her toes. She planted a long, luscious kiss on his lips. Slightly shocked, he gripped her by the shoulders, keeping a proper distance. She pulled her head back and looked quizzically at him for a moment, as though expecting him to say or do something else. He stood there like a block of stone as people whooped and blew party horns all around him.

The band launched into a raucous version of Auld Lang Syne, played in his honour he assumed. Some classmates came and dragged Francesca to the dance floor. As he was dragged in a different direction, he saw Francesca looking back over her shoulder as if there were more to be said. But the moment to say it was gone.

The kiss was one of several from his female students and colleagues that night but Francesca's kiss was different from the others. A challenge, not just a nervous peck. But then, she *was* different. Even so, he convinced himself that it didn't mean anything. It was just a bit of over-enthusiasm from the usually super-cool Francesca.

« »

"Anybody home?" he shouted cheerily as he came through the front door. The cheerfulness was more in hope than expectation.

James could have predicted the reply. He mouthed the words silently as Lisa spat them at him from the lounge:

"And what time do you call this?"

He threw his keys onto the hall table, dropped his rugby kit by the door and went to look in the fridge. Beer always left him ravenous:

"I'm always late when we play away. You know that. I called into the club-house for one final drink and, you know, one thing led to another. Anyway, I'm home now."

He entered the lounge, crumbs from the piece of quiche he'd found cascading down his front. Oh my God! She was smartly dressed and made-up ready to go out. He didn't think he'd forgotten anything. Birthday? Anniversary? No. Nothing popped into his head.

"Are we going out?"

"I thought if you'd come home early enough, we could have gone for a meal to the Bistro. As a couple for once. But you obviously prefer your boozy mates to your girlfriend." She switched channels. A repeat soap was just starting.

"Look. I've just had a few beers with the boys after a hard match. Is that too much once a week?"

"And after training. And after golf. And at the tennis club. Balls and beer! That's all you're bothered about. You're thirty eight, for God's sake. You should grow up, be thinking about other things than chasing leather balls around a field and coming home crocked. A career. Commitment. Children even. Grown-up things!"

His heart didn't sink at this Saturday night ritual. It was already sunk. He'd had enough. So had she. Even the arguments were just going through the motions. There was no venom in them anymore.

It was a wonder to their friends that the relationship had lasted as long as it had. Mary and James knew themselves that there was no future in it. They'd never shown much commitment. Theirs was a very dividable relationship. It was as if, throughout the whole eleven years, their cases had been half-packed, ready for the parting of the ways that was now upon them.

The early years had been pleasant enough. They were sexually attracted to one another and enjoyed going out together to see and be seen. They'd moved in together quickly and rented their small house, sharing every cost meticulously.

She had no interest in his sport and he liked to keep that to himself. She was into Facebook, shopping, lunching with her girl-friends. They'd made few compromises on their previous lives as single people and ever fewer demands on one another as time went on. Of course, they'd never married or even seriously considered it. With hindsight (and perhaps even with a bit of foresight), this had saved them the cost of a divorce as well as a wedding.

Finally, the pointlessness of staying together could be ignored no longer. The moment of separation was rapidly approaching. James would move to a rented flat in a town about eight miles from where they lived now. He had taught at a nearby college since his return some years earlier from working in Rome. Most of his social contacts were in the area, mainly his drinking mates from the tennis, golf and rugby clubs, where he spent a lot of his free time.

« »

So, fourteen years on from his time in Rome, he sat in the study of the home he was giving up, dividing books and CDs into 'his' and 'hers' piles. He'd come to the section of the shelves that contained his books and other bits and bobs from Italy. They were clearly all his property so the allocation was simple. What was delaying him was the compulsion to dip into the books and to handle the little mementoes that released the genie of his earlier life.

He was staring, eyes glazed, at one of the few books in Italian: "*Va' dove ti porta il cuore*" by Susanna Tamaro. It had been given to him as a leaving present by one of his classes and was signed on the inside page by all the students. He'd never read the book. In fact he'd never even read the inscriptions inside the front cover properly. He'd felt sad to be leaving this group of likeable young people. He'd thanked them awkwardly and wished them all well. Later, he'd rather casually thrown the book into his bag in preparation for leaving for England for the final time. The book had subsequently made its way, unread, onto every book-shelf he'd had.

He paused to make himself a cup of the strong, sweet espresso he'd come to love in his time in Rome. He returned to the study, sat down in the swivel chair, picked up the book and started to decipher all the individual names on the inside cover. He tried to call up all the faces that he'd seen every day of his last six months at the college. He was able to conjure up a face for most of the names…

"God Go with You!" Elena…She was the shy, devout girl. Very conscientious, bright and sweet but who melted away when class finished, only to re-appear at the start of the next lesson;

"Good Luck…Return Some Day" Luca…the clerk working in his uncle's import-export firm;

"Cheers!"…Bruno, the gregarious young man who was behind many of the outings.

There were some faces he could not recall but the final name, oddly apart from the rest at the bottom of the page, was the most memorable…

… from Francesca, XXX…

Francesca was the only one he had thought about over the years. He had remembered her midnight-kiss on every New Years Eve since leaving Rome.

He stared down at her distinctive, florid signature. Below it, he noticed another shape for the first time. She'd drawn a neat heart symbol. What an oaf he was never to have looked at all of this properly! Within the shape of the heart were two tiny numbers, one in either chamber…a four and a seven. How odd. He stared out of the window, wondering what the numbers could mean.

He turned hopefully to page forty seven in the book. There, across the top of the page, was a string of neat numbers… 0039 06 61 48387.

What an idiot. It was a number for which half the youth of Rome would have given a small ransom. How could he have missed the other signs that there must have been? What must Francesca have made of his silence? Francesca would have been reason enough to stay in Rome and to give up the half-baked plans he'd had. His life could have been so different.

The book slipped from his grasp. He slumped lower in the chair, propped his head on one hand. He sat there for a few minutes.

Perhaps it wasn't too late. Was there a chance she was still there and still thought of him? He became agitated.

It was ridiculous to expect that she'd waited fourteen years for this idiot Englishman to finally crack the riddle. She would have had many relationships, offers of marriage, no doubt of that. But what if these hadn't worked out and she'd found herself alone again? Maybe the number was still the same. Her parents had owned a substantial home in a lovely part of the city. She may have inherited the house, or even returned there if her marriage had broken down. There was a chance…slim… but a chance nonetheless. Stranger things happened. People sometimes met up again many years after parting because of misunderstandings or the workings of fate.

The prize was tremendous. The chance both to move on and to move back, to re-wind to a time when he and life still had possibilities. A chance to re-invent the young man he'd once been and to put the dullard he'd become behind him.

He had nothing to lose. He might face a 'James who moment?' Embarrassed confusion. A swift rejection. Nothing worse.

He drained the last of his coffee. He picked the book up. It fell open at the title page where the spine was broken. Someone had translated the title for him: "*Follow Your Heart.*" It was of course Francesca's distinctive hand.

He turned back to page forty seven and broke the spine again so it stayed open on the desk in front of him. His hand snaked out towards the phone but stopped a few inches short as his eyes focused on Francesca's number. His heart began to pound faster than it had done for years. He dialled the first zero. He continued methodically to the final seven.

It took an age to connect and then several rings before it was answered.

"Francesca Mancini. Pronto. Chai parla?"

"Hello! Francesca? It's James. James Roberts… I used to teach you English at your college…"

Silence. A long silence.

He heard a male voice in the background: "Chi ė?"

His recalled the meaning of the man's curt phrase: "Who is it?"

He waited for Francesca to answer, either him or the male voice. The answer was to both.

"Nessuno. Absolutely nobody."

The Funeral Director

I feel nothing. I am dead. Cold and numb as stone, although I can't *feel* cold or numbness. I can't bruise, hurt or feel anything in any physical way. Even so, I am still relieved that I'm not sliding around in the coffin as I am borne down the aisle to the front of the crematorium. I am pleased I've not been tipped to one end of the coffin because of course I no longer have any control over my tendons, bones and muscle. I simply wouldn't be able to shuffle my bony backside back into its proper position in the coffin. Very undignified that would be on this of all days.

It's clever how they've fixed me in here, tight in the satin lining so I can't roll with the motion as they glide forward and place me down on the bier. Naturally the *dead* bit, as in *dead weight*, also helps keeps me still.

Not sliding about in the coffin is only part of my contentment. Most of all, I feel relief that all the planning has been worthwhile. I'm going to enjoy myself today. In fact, I am already enjoying myself in my quiet way. I have so looked forward to this day. *My* day and I don't want there to be any distractions…no bumps or thudding noises against the coffin sides…to divert my guests from their job today, mourning. I want to be dispatched according to the plan I've made for this, my cremation, the only party I've ever held in my life.

« »

The diagnosis had been a shock. It had devastated both Jane and me initially. But that devastation had not lasted. I'd known as soon as the consultant told me it was cancer that I would not be cured. It would kill me, sooner rather than later.

Mr Bramwell-Jones made the usual attempts to give hope. But, as good a doctor as he might be, he was a poor actor. His eyes let him down at crucial moments, drifting away from their connection with mine. He'd no doubt practiced switching on the sincere look at the point when things were most fraught. But you can't hide it when one person knows something so important about the person in front of him but he himself doesn't. That he will die, soon and possibly painfully.

"It's a form of cancer that's really quite amenable to a number of treatments" he said, emphasising the word 'number'.

This was a finely-balanced statement, calibrated to let people project onto it the meaning they could cope with. I chose my own meaning. Your senses are sharp when your life's at issue. You're so attuned, so prickly with sensitivity, that you glimpse the real meaning, the one lurking behind the actual words used.

The 'really' was overkill but the 'quite' was purposely ambiguous. Mr Bramwell-Jones meant '*fairly* amenable', but he wanted me to understand '*very* amenable'. The more I mulled over that particular sentence in the weeks to come, lying awake at night, replaying every word and gesture, the more it confirmed my initial judgment. His words were literally a death sentence. Once I'd concluded that, there was no way it couldn't happen.

Jane had hung onto 'very amenable' much longer than me. She'd also clutched onto the idea of 'a number of treatments' as meaning a wealth of escape routes. Blind alleys more like it. There was no escape. I could almost smell it in the consulting room, in the demeanour of the staff at the hospital, and then at my own surgery where everyone suddenly became nice and helpful. Jane, too, had gradually accepted that I was going to die.

Eventually, we started to make adjustments. Weirdly, as I weakened physically, my will to take control strengthened. As my physical world contracted down to the bed I spent my time in, the more influence I exerted on those around me. My needs and wishes dominated everything.

« »

I was luxuriating in the enveloping bed that we'd bought to make this final period of my life more comfortable. I rolled over from my side and came to rest on my back with my hands cupped smugly beneath my head. It wasn't just the bed that was contributing to my well-being. It was mid-morning and the nurse had recently given me my pain relief. I was clean, shaved, rested, without pain. Well, actually with a mild feeling of euphoria. With Jane out, I had peace and quiet and the comfort of my big bed to lie and snooze and enjoy the morphine before its power ebbed and the pain returned.

The decision to lash out on the best bed money could buy was part of the new-thinking that Jane and I had developed in response to the fact that, at forty-one, I'd now finally been told that I wouldn't make forty-two. What's more, the time left to me would be pretty brutish. Comforts might be rare.

At any time in the years B.C., (*Before Cancer*, as we came to call that earlier period of our lives), we'd have debated buying a new bed for weeks. We were careful people. Anyway, I thought I had thirty years or so ahead of me, so where was the rush? But now we hadn't time to mess about. If I didn't do it immediately, that was it. Every opportunity was a last chance. At death's door, I'd never been more capable of deciding what I wanted to do with my life. And the first thing I'd decided I wanted to do was to sleep out my nights and die in a decent bed.

One of the real benefits the cancer had brought me was that it simplified things so much. So many choices were taken from me. Changing jobs. Going for promotion. Moving house. Changing cars. Wondering. Worrying. Well, no more.

The months I had were too important to be taken up with such complete irrelevances. All wind and fury really, a fart, signifying nothing. The real puzzle was why I'd ever thought such things important at all. What a waste of time! Precious time. Time not to be squandered as if there was an endless supply of it. Time that could be spent on important things.

Yes, I had my cancer to thank for simplifying things beautifully.

« »

The shallowness of people who didn't realise that every day could be their last became laughable to me even as they did me the kindness of visiting. Few friends and colleagues had the guts to come and see me now that I was so frail, an old man at forty one. A still-live cadaver that no-one could pretend would get better.

I didn't mind so much for myself. I felt quite ill more of the time and got tired and irritated quite quickly. But I knew that Jane needed some distraction. They could have come more often for her sake. I knew I alienated some of them, selfishly, not considering the way it added to Jane's isolation and would make things harder for her once I was gone. But I couldn't help it. There was a compulsion to say it if I thought it, rude or not, because I wouldn't get another chance.

The visitors I did get talked about their own lives or their work because my life was not such a great conversation piece any longer. It all seemed trivial with me facing what was before me. Some of them knew it. They felt awkward, shallow, spoilt, even guilty.

Others were vain. They still thought it couldn't happen to them. As if I must have somehow deserved it or been weak or something. As if they were different, made of sterner stuff. Or with a constitution that would survive a pile-up on the M1. And so, thinking they were indestructible, they still lived as if they had an age before them. They squandered their time on the old irrelevances. I was contemptuous of these more than any others.

Jane would try to get rid of them diplomatically if she knew I was in one of my honest moods. She had to go on living with them but I had no need for tact.

"No. I am *not* in pain!" I'd shout down the stairs to correct her. "Tell him the truth. I simply don't want to spend half of one of my remaining hours talking about his kids, his mortgage or even his frigging sports car! I'm not interested in 0-60 in 7.5 seconds, because in 0-6 months I'll be dead!"

I paused to shuffle my bony backside in bed. "Tell the boring fart to sod off! And tell him not to come to the funeral!"

Jane had no need to tell him. My voice carried still.

"It's OK, Jane. I understand," drifted up the stairs.

I was waiting for it.

"No you bloody well don't understand. You don't even understand that you don't understand. That's your problem! You don't understand anything that actually matters."

Jane would cringe and usher them out. They'd pad quietly down the drive, relieved to have been absolved of further responsibility. They could say they'd tried. "But so bitter towards the end," they'd explain to one another. "So hard to reach."

A blistering honesty was this tumour's second gift.

« »

They needn't have felt embarrassed. I wasn't jealous. I didn't want their concerns and worries. I had my own agenda. It was bigger, more urgent, more real. B.C., I'd always been absolutely emasculated by the minutiae of life. It had obsessed me and controlled my life utterly. I wore myself out in pursuit of trivia all day long, and then fretted all night over the unfinished business of the day. In my B.C. years, if God had given me a choice between, say, painting a universally-acclaimed Masterpiece of Twenty First Century Art or completing routine trivial tasks, then there would have been absolutely no choice for me. I would have had to empty the dish-washer, wash the car, mow the lawn and tidy the garage first, before devoting the fag-end of the day to getting out the oils and the easel. Displacement behaviour, the psychologists called it. I had been the master. But not any more. I was now free of that neurosis, too.

Yes, it was a great healer, this tumour, in its own way.

I had the big agenda, now. It was about paring away the lies and falsehoods and making some clear statements about love and hate and faithfulness and weakness. It was about settling scores and healing hurts.

I had always been faithful to Jane. I had to be sure that her belief was rock-solid and she wasn't saying she believed me because she wanted to protect me from her doubts at this final stage.

I also tried to talk to her about life after death. Not in a religious sense, more about her life after my death. It was too painful for her. She'd leave the room. Shut herself off.

She didn't want to hear it but I ploughed on, as soon as another chance arose, bullying her to listen. But this was good bullying. I wanted her to know that she should have all choices in life available to her once I was gone. She deserved it. She had been so devoted, so caring, so brave. She would have no debt to me after the service. She didn't need to die with me. I knew she didn't want to hear, but I hoped that if the words were said, she could return to them at an easier time and see them for what they were, my 'Thank you', a message of love.

« »

Weak as I was becoming physically, my family and remaining friends had never seen such determination in me. It seemed to humble the people closest to me and make them submissive. What power dying had given me over my life and those around me! Knowing the approximate time and nature of my own death was like knowing how a book ends, having the last chapter read to me, and then being given the opportunity to write the intervening chapters. One of these intervening chapters was my funeral service.

Many people still avoid considering their own funerals. I'd never thought much about it B.C. This neglect is a shame really. Life's last party but we often leave it poorly thought-out and de-personalised. Taking control of my own funeral was part of my new approach to life once I knew my illness was terminal. I was running out of time.

I needed to make sure events did not happen around me, with me a passive observer.

With my new-found strength, no one had dared oppose my funeral plan as it developed. I was the one dying early. It was my pain. They were not going to deny me…not Jane, not the vicar, not the funeral director. None of them. It was going to be just as I wanted. I was signing people up to it. Who would deny a man so obviously dying? I'd had them all in and eyeballed them. There'd be no backsliding from any of them.

In any case, what I wanted was not so extravagant. Quite modest really. Basically a conventional package but customised a bit. That was all.

Firstly, I wanted as much fuss and show as possible. I wanted no creep in, bury him and creep out job, with everyone tippy-toeing about and speaking in whispers. I'd always envied these Gypsy funerals. A long cortège and plenty of noise. Or Irish wakes, when ructions would break out. At least something happened, a ripple on the serene surface of life and death. I wouldn't get ructions from my family and friends but I might get a house and church full with a bit of effort.

I'd written a notice to go quickly into the local newspapers, both where I would die and where I was brought up. I'd also done a brief obituary for the same papers. These should let people know in time to get to the funeral. I'd given Jane a circulation list for e-mail notification of acquaintances and colleagues. Well, those I hadn't banned in one of my tirades.

I wanted a horse-drawn carriage, with a top-hatted funeral director leading the way. Sorry. I meant Assistant Director, subordinate to me obviously.

I wanted as many flowers as people were prepared to pay for. This was extravagance I'd never shown in life, although of course in this instance it was extravagance with other people's money.

I expected as a minimum some serious crying. The music had been selected to achieve this, traditional for the church and more personalised for the crematorium.

An old friend of mine, Pete, has been learning the Irish bag-pipes. We'd drunk hard to Irish music as young men in my short-lived wild phase. His wild phase had never ended, which is why we only met annually to catch up. It was as much wildness as I could stand now I was respectable and equally as much respectability as Pete could cope with. He was, however, one of the few able to talk with me honestly about my impending death. He was keen to hear my plans and even to play a part.

We came up with the idea of me being piped into the crematorium with a lament we both liked called *The Lonesome Boatman*. Pete's pipe-playing still left a bit to be desired and the pipes are an unforgiving sound if not played right. Pete agreed to rehearse this one song as much as he could in the time available. If he made the grade, he would pipe me into the crematorium. He felt he could be near perfect if I could live just a little longer than scheduled. We agreed four months should do it.

Pete must have really thrown himself into the practice because after just two months I got a text from him that said simply: "Ready when you are. Pete."

I liked that. Someone keen to help realise my plan, not talk me out of it.

One other important piece of music was a secret statement of what Jane had meant to me and the loss, the only real one I felt, at leaving her. She would understand. We'd listened in silence to the song together in the car or at home, knowing what part it would play on the day.

I wanted my lifelong friend to read John Donne's '*No man is an Island*'. Was it socialism, humanitarianism, Christianity? I had always flip-flopped between the three. I'd given up trying to pin it down. It meant what it meant and to me, it was about our responsibility for each other. It spoke of how I'd tried to live my life.

I stopped short of writing the eulogy. I am not a control freak after all. Not normally. I knew it would reflect how I had wanted to be seen anyway, with my weaknesses and foibles airbrushed out, or referred to as amusing eccentricities when in fact they'd been infuriating.

The exit from the crematorium was to be accompanied by brass band music. There shouldn't be a dry eye in the house.

That would be enough. A conventional package, but with some personal touches. Not much to ask.

« »

Of course, the only thing I could not know with any certainly from the living side of death, your side that is, was whether I would know whether the plan was followed or not. That remains a mystery for those of you still alive. It is unknowable for you but not, now, for me.

As I'm being shuffled down the aisle, with weeping around me, I'm delighted to share with you that I am aware. I'm more than aware. I am in control of it all still. It is as I planned it.

The church service set the mood. Pete was brilliant just now with the pipes. Really moving. If I could have, I would have cried. I'll forgive him the fact that he's nipped off to the pub, not followed me in. Anyway, he's done me proud.

I sense who's mourning and who is not. Who's thinking of how quickly they can get away. Who's thinking fondly of me and things we did together. Who's feeling respect and sadness. Tomorrow they can all happily get on with their lives with my blessing, every one of them, Jane included. Especially Jane for all she has put up with. All I'd like is that, very occasionally, they will remember me and smile. But today I am happy to know that they are sad.

As I lie at the front of the crematorium in my final earthly moments, I can no longer intervene in the events around me. I can't pull any more strings. I wouldn't want to. I've done enough. I'm tired. Spent. Nonetheless, I am happy finally that it is how I wanted it to be. My work is done. I can rest.

Lullaby

February, 2010: the Front Room of an Older Person's Bungalow in York.

The social worker is *still* talking. I thought I could talk. But this one could talk for England.

"We've got you down as Isabela with one 'l'. That can't be right, Mrs Appleyard? Should it be double 'l'?"

"Yes, two 'ls'. Isabella. It was my family's favourite girl's name. Every first-born girl was Isabella."

"Mm. Interesting."

Interesting or not, he didn't look up from his forms. He changed the subject:

"So, that's agreed, then, Isabella. Mrs. Appleyard, I mean. You'll move into Peppermill Court on Saturday for a week's assessment. And then you'll probably stay on for some rehab for a few weeks."

He's talking loud again. He knows I'm deaf. He wrote it down last time he came. Not sure writing it down on a bit of paper helps. I'm still deaf.

Even when I can hear, I don't understand half these newfangled words. Rehab? Assessment? Everything needs *assessing* nowadays. Nobody knows what to do straight away. They talk to their colleagues about you so everyone ends up knowing you wet yourself. Then they do what was obvious at the start. Give you some pads and pants. Well, put you on a waiting list for them until you give in and buy some yourself.

No. Nobody knows their job anymore. Not like the old days when the Doctor told you: "Do this! Take that!" And you did it and got better.

Or not. Not when you're 94. Or am I 95? I'm not sure.

And as for all these therapists! Everyone's a therapist now. *Physioterrorists* we call them at the Centre. They pretend you can go on forever. They're all so blooming cheery! Mildred, my friend at the centre, her son told her that physiotherapists are too stupid to be doctors and too posh to be nurses. She was telling me what he'd said. Only Mildred was having to shout it to me with me being deaf and one of them heard her. Face like thunder for the rest of the afternoon. Anyway, they think you're not really trying if you don't want to go mountaineering at a hundred. They won't be so cheery when it's them that's old.

I've done well, really. Still at home long after most have gone into care homes or popped their clogs. Alone for the past eighteen years since Mr. Appleyard died.

But age still gets you no matter how much blooming rehab they force down your throat. You just get very tired in the end. And bored. Rolling those balls to one another in a big circle of wheelchairs at the Centre! How's that help a failing heart and a brain drying out like winter leaves?

I'm drifting off. I know it. I do it more and more. My mind just floats off where it wants. Got a mind of its own, you could say.

He's *still* talking at me:

"…then we'll decide, with you of course, what happens next."

I'm not daft. I know what "decide, *with you*…" means. It means they'll ask me my opinion and then do what *they* want.

"You may need somewhere to move onto permanently if you can't look after yourself. We need to keep you safe, what with the falls and the wandering outside at night and the burned pans."

That stuff doesn't worry me like it does everyone else. What does that girl on the telly say? "Am I bovvered?" No I'm not. My memory's letting me down. But I'm only forgetting silly things. Things that aren't important. I still remember stuff from my earlier life. My real life. I re-live that daily. Starting school. Wedding day. My own little Isabella being born…and dying, still little. The important things.

A burned pan. So what? Putting the pan on the cooker was just a foggy memory. I'd have denied doing it if the evidence hadn't been there for all to see, blackened and burned out. Guilty as charged. But that isn't where I live anymore. I live in those pictures of my earlier life.

He does go on!

"Ok. I give in," I blurt out. "I'll give this Court place a go,"

He stops mid-sentence. He looks as if he's won a raffle.

"Such fancy names these places have. Who thinks them up, the fancy names?" I ask.

He doesn't reply. He's fiddling in his bag for more papers…the 'get-her-in quick' papers I suppose. His pen flies across the forms, trying to get them complete before I change my mind. It's nice to make someone happy.

29th August, 1839. Meeting of Workhouse Guardians, Huntingdon Road, York. Williams Smithson, Chair of the Board of Guardians Presiding; Item 5: Mr W. White, Chemist, is addressing the Board on the cause of a fatal outbreak of sickness

I shuffle my backside in the captain's chair but find no comfort. As Chairman of the Board, I could expect something more commodious. It's a bit tight for a man of my girth.

It's this discussion that's causing me most discomfort though. All this talk of putrefaction, excrement, vomiting and the like. Really! I must speak to the Clerk. How idiotic of him to put this recent epidemic on the agenda immediately after lunch. And such a good lunch at that. The pie and the gooseberry tart were particular highlights. So tasty going down but the game pie is now like a great stone in my stomach. It'll take some digesting if this report goes on much longer.

Bad business this epidemic. A disaster for the accounts. God knows what all this extra cleaning will cost. The

Master's bringing in help at great expense to cope with the work. Most of the inmates are now incapable of work or indeed of anything other than spewing all day long.

Three deaths already. Three poor, sickly wretches for the most part. What were their names? Down here somewhere in these papers:

Bertram Johnson	53
Elijah Morton	29
Isabella Holroyd	23

Thank God no infants. Something to be grateful for.

Many of the surviving inmates are lying in their own filth. Nothing new in that. Isn't that how they are habituated to living at home. This present squalor is just their usual way. At least it's concentrated in one spot here in the workhouse, not spread through the whole City. Thank God we can't smell the stench here in the Board Room.

Mmm. I can see from their tight-lipped expressions and frequent shuffling just how much this business irritates my fellow Guardians. Still, we need to hear this fellow out even if he is going on a bit for my liking.

We Guardians give our time, more or less willingly, to ensure prudent administration of the City's poor law duties. There's little reward or praise in it for us. Yes, we have the chance to do a bit of business on the side, quietly. I myself supply furniture and basic bedding from one of my concerns. At a very good price. For the Workhouse that is. Guardian Booth's company does repairs. Johnson supplies foodstuff, including the meat that this damnable chemist-fellow, White, is suggesting was the probable cause of the outbreak.

Do get a move on White! Are all chemists so damnably long-winded?

Well, we do our best with the monies allowed us. Our primary duty is to stop the costs to rate-paying citizens getting out of hand. Our second is to stop life in the workhouse getting so comfortable that it becomes ever more attractive to the indolent rogues flocking to York from the surrounding villages and beyond. No, my Board is not prepared to let the workhouse become a magnet for the rest of the country's ne'er-do-wells. Over my dead body!

The cheek of this White fellow. Doesn't seem to know whose side he's on. He's confidently ruled out poison as cause of the illness. He's not holding back in his report:

"…I found, Gentleman, an arrangement for the preparation of food that was extremely hazardous to health, especially of the young and the infirm. I have concluded that the kitchen is totally ill-adapted for the cooking of food."

He's a decent speaker, I suppose. Give him that. He's not using notes. And he's got our attention alright now. Good, he's summing up. Won't be long now.

"Firstly, I found a beast's head offensive to the smell. In spite of its state of decomposition, the Master informed me that it would not be cooked for several days.

Unwholesome mucus was emanating from it. It is not known exactly what state the flesh used in the suspect soup was in when it was cooked. The evidence has now disappeared down the privies. However, if it was similar to the beast-head I saw, it is almost certainly the cause of the epidemic."

Johnson, the meat purveyor, is glaring at White.

I find myself shuffling again. The game pie is repeating on me terribly. I fear I'm going to vomit. The taste has risen to the back of my throat like a reek from the workhouse privies. I gulp and it abates.

"Secondly," White continues, "the kitchen opens onto an enclosed yard with privies at the other side at a distance of only six yards. The air is tainted by the effluvia from these privies. The yard is a permanent reservoir of foul air."

His expression darkens:

"Thirdly, there is a clear lack of ventilation in relation to the numbers accommodated. This means that such an outbreak as has occurred will spread with speed, even to those inmates not subject to primary contamination by the noxious material."

He pauses. He says, matter-of-factly:

"Gentlemen, my inevitable conclusion is that urgent and far-reaching reforms are needed. I shall be sending my report to the Poor Law Commissioners as a matter of urgency."

White sits down and awaits a response. Silence.

I invite questions.

Johnson speaks first, as planned.

"Through the chair, Mr. White," he whines. "I'd like to ask you if you know how much food allowance we are given for each inmate."

White's cheeks flush a little.

"I do not know that, Sir. That is not my business. I was invited to give my opinion on the cause of the outbreak. That I have done. It seems clear that the insanitary conditions are its cause. Indeed, I am also of the opinion that this should have been clear to any member of this Board blessed with a reasonable olfactory function. You would, I believe, have saved yourselves my fee by taking a tour of the building and scenting the air as you went along."

There's a sharp intake of breath, as if someone had opened the door to the privy yard and the sour smell had wafted into our nostrils.

We are invulnerable, though. We just have to stick together. Our next question, mine, is measured:

"The usual scientific way, I understand, is to develop a range of hypotheses and evaluate the evidence for each. You have already excluded poison as the cause, Mr. White. Did you consider any other hypothesis?"

"I did not, Sir. The cause was plain as a pike-staff," he replies.

"You see," I continue, "We have not been tardy, as you seem to think. We have considered other possibilities. We have looked into the matter at length, in private. It is our belief, based on many years experience of the paupers and feeble-minded of York, that the problem is self-induced. It arises largely from the lifelong habits of the inmates of our institution. This is a…a…species that we know rather better than you, no matter how long you have studied chemistry."

"What can you mean, Mr. Smithson? Why would anyone inflict such an ordeal on themselves or, more unthinkably, on their infants?" asks White."How are these people to blame?"

I proceed, slowly and deliberately:

"These *people*, as you delicately call them, don't think like you or I, White. They have no knowledge of diet, health or temperate conduct. Outside the workhouse, they prefer to spend their money on gin and ale rather than on wholesome food. The Master told you during your inspection that on the day in question, the soup served immediately before the outbreak of the epidemic was unusually full of flesh and nourishing fat. The inmates simply could not digest so rich and wholesome a meal, hence their rampant sickness. Our kindness and bounty is the cause. It is as simple as that. We are surprised that a learned man such as you has overlooked this finding."

White is thrown but only for a few seconds.

"Sir, your finding is preposterous," he finally replies.

The rest of the Board clucks away in support of my point but White is unmoved:

"No evidence supports it. That is why I dismissed it. If the epidemic were a response to the richness of the stew, why has it persisted so long? Why have inmates not partaking of the suspect meal also been struck down? It is the combination of contaminated food and the generally unsanitary conditions that have produced this tragedy. I am not prepared to simply present to you the opinion you desire and then to charge you a fee for it. The matter is too important for that."

White pauses, gathers himself and resumes:

"Others know much better, more modern ways in this City of ours. At the Retreat Asylum, not two miles from here, wonders have been achieved when inmates enjoy sanitary conditions and the kindness that all God's creatures deserve. Improvements here in Huntingdon Road Workhouse need to start from that premise, Gentlemen. I can arrange a visit to the Retreat if you wish. Tomorrow..."

I cut him dead. I speak without looking at him.

"Thank you! That won't be required. We are too busy for excursions. And you have done quite enough. We thank you for your report, Sir, and bid you Good Day. We will discuss the matter further in private."

White half forms a reply, thinks better of it, puts on his hat and coat, picks up his cane and leaves us to our business without a backward look.

Our deliberations are short. The Board formally records that the epidemic had been caused by the richness of the soup.

Back in the Bungalow

He's finished the forms, in record-time probably. He's put a big X where I have to sign. He gives me a really thick pen that's easy to grip.

"It's especially made for people with arthritis," he says.

"You think of everything," I reply.

My bony fingers clutch the fat pen. My hand is shaking slightly as the pen hovers over the X.

"So where in York is it, this Peppermint Court?" I ask.

"Peppermill... Pepper*mill* Court," he replies, still ferreting in his bag. "It's on Huntington Road. Don't worry. We'll get you there."

My ears prick up at that address. It's a road I've known since childhood. Not known, exactly. Heard-of more like. We'd all heard of it, whether we'd been in it or not.

"Where on Huntington Road?"

He thinks I'm keen. He's wrong.

"It's where the Grange Hospital used to be. And there were other welfare establishments there, way back before that, back into the 19th century. Back even to the York Workhouse, I think. It's a lovely new building now and..."

I don't hear the end of his sentence. I'm drifting off again. A street-rhyme from my childhood wafts into my mind, more vivid than burning pans or wanderings in the garden at night:

"Hush-a-bye Baby, on a Tree-top;
When you grow old, your Wages will stop.
When you have spent the Little you made,
First to the Workhouse and then to the Grave."

"I'm not going," I say, handing back his pen and flopping back into my chair. And I don't.